Bolan launched his silent death-stalk...

With ice eyes he moved through the darkness.

He was brother to the forest. He could sense the positions of the enemy guards scattered there.

He visited them one by one. Without noise or light or argument, he dispatched them. He laid each knifed carcass on the forest floor.

In the camp below, a surviving sentry lit a cigarette.

The night-knifer picked up an M-16 from a fallen guard, checked the selector, and called out softly, "Up here."

The guy's head snapped around—in time to take a 5.56 mm bonecrusher in the face.

Mack Bolan's
ABLE TEAM

#1 Tower of Terror
#2 The Hostaged Island
#3 Texas Showdown

Mack Bolan's
PHOENIX FORCE

#1 Argentine Deadline
#2 Guerilla Games
#3 Atlantic Scramble

MACK BOLAN

THE EXECUTIONER 50

BOLAN

Brothers in Blood

A GOLD EAGLE BOOK FROM

W☉RLDWIDE

TORONTO · NEW YORK · LONDON

First edition February 1983

ISBN 0-373-61050-5

Special thanks and acknowledgment to
Steven Krauzer for his contributions to this work.

Printed in Canada

Tomorrow is the most important thing in life.
Comes into us at midnight very clean.
It is perfect when it arrives
and it puts itself into our hands.
It hopes we've learned something from yesterday.
>   —*John Wayne*

>   ...What, then, is your duty?
> Only this: whatever the day demands!
>   —*Goethe*

My brother Johnny—I pray that you go safe
in this world, and that you bring courage
to every moment. Act well for now
and you perform a good deed for eternity.
Courage is the good stuff that guarantees all else.
>   —*Mack Bolan, The Executioner*
>   (from his correspondence)

THE PRESIDENT

Hal —

    A personal note. I want you
to get John Phoenix to lie low.
NSC tells me the KGB is
infiltrating world terrorist network
in order to hit <u>Phoenix</u>.

    Loss of this man would be a
tragic blow to us, impossible to
rectify. I know you appreciate this.

PROLOGUE

Mack Bolan neither asked for nor expected tangible reward. As a U.S. Army sergeant in Vietnam, he fought because his country needed him. His skills were required to help preserve the precarious world balance to which the great democratic superpower was a primary contributor. Later, as a blitzing crusader against the omnipresent specter of organized crime, he fought to eradicate the invidious blight that had infected the society of that same noble country.

Now Mack Bolan was director of the Stony Man Operation for the Sensitive Operations Group of the National Security Council, answerable only to the man in the Oval Office. His new mandate was to combat the vicious, ubiquitous terrorist groups taking root and sprouting around the globe. As always, the enemy was sworn to anarchy and oppression; as always, Bolan was sworn to the preservation of freedom, equality, true justice.

Although he was aware of the sacrifices involved in the life he had freely chosen, Bolan did not dwell on them. His war would continue until the day the savages who preyed on the gentle people were eradicated from the face of the planet.

But history, and his personal understanding that he was hardly a superman, told Bolan that day would be long in coming.

Mack Bolan's kind of war would stop only when he himself was stopped—permanently.

In the meantime the Vietnam War, the Mafia war, now the terrorist wars were consuming his life, occupying and dominating his every waking minute.

Today the jackals can with impunity attack the president-elect of Lebanon, the president of Egypt, even the supreme pontiff. So who can be safe? Somewhere in the world, horrific depredations take place daily.

So for Bolan, the end of one mission only meant the beginning of another. On the rare occasions when his respite lasted even a few days, he spent that time going over Intelligence data on the terrorist threat, researching the interconnections of the global terrorist network, intensively learning all he could about his enemy. The success of his war and the preservation of his life depended on one-hundred-percent dedication.

And that is why Mack Bolan, seated in the War Room of his Stony Man Farm headquarters, was stunned at the suggestion that had just been so strongly put to him.

"A vacation?" he repeated, incredulous.

"At least give it some thought," Hal Brognola insisted. The somewhat sad-faced middle-aged man who sat across the conference table from Bolan puffed blue cigar smoke into the War Room's oppressive dimness. He looked like an overworked business executive. In fact he was the major wheel in the Department of Justice and was Bolan's liaison with the president himself. From the early days of the Mafia war, Brognola had reluctantly given Bolan covert assistance, from simple nonintervention to tactical support. At first, his secret alliance with the most wanted man in America went against everything the born-to-the-harness lawman believed in. Yet he came to realize that The Executioner's brand of direct action—the Bolan Effect, as it was called by cops and vermin alike—was the only method that had ever succeeded in the decades-old campaign against the organized scum that was devouring the infrastructure of the country like termites in a lumberyard.

"Hal is right," April Rose agreed. "It's more important than just taking a break. It could be crucial to everything we're working for." She opened a manila folder on the table in front of her and glanced at the top sheet. "Studies have shown that regular and continual exposure to stressful situations, without a break or change of pace, can reduce a person's efficiency—" she consulted her data again "—by as much as two-thirds."

The auburn-haired beauty with that improbable last name, Rose, so beautiful a name to Bolan's ears, had joined The Executioner at the beginning of the last six days of his first holy crusade, days that saw the final vestiges of the Mafia beast sicken and die. A federal agent, a ballistics expert, a trained physicist and computer scientist—and an incredibly beautiful young woman—she was now in charge of operations at Stony Man, the Executioner's HQ complex in the shadow of Virginia's Blue Ridge Mountains.

She wore a jump suit that accentuated her generous curves, its front zipper stopping low enough to tantalizingly preview what the rest of her promised.

"Don't take this wrong, Mack," she said gently, "but even *you* can't expect to operate at your peak every moment of every day. You remember what happened in London."

Yeah, Bolan remembered London. While on the trail of renegade ex-CIA agent Frank Edwards, he had been shot in the shoulder—ironically, by a British agent who did not realize that Bolan was a soldier of the same side. Like other recent wounds, it was not long-term serious, and it was now healed— but another three inches lower and it could have been fatal.

Bolan had been wounded too many times to dwell on this incident, so he had chalked it up to battlefield luck and forgotten it. And yet...maybe April had something. . . .

"Whether or not you are willing to admit it, Mack Bolan, you are human. And you have been on mission alert eleven times already since our Stony Man Operation was inaugurated. And Libya was truly terrible. It made a killing machine out of you, however necessary. That was Edge City, Mack, strictly terror to an insane degree in my opinion. . . ."

"April, the world is at war. I can't afford to—"

"You can't afford *not* to rest up," April interrupted. "Think of us, of everything we've built here. If you don't give yourself a break, someone or something is going to break you, sooner or later. That is fact, Mister Blitz."

"Easy," Hal cautioned softly.

She shook her head angrily. Bolan understood; he knew the depth of her feeling for him and returned it in equal measure.

"I'm sorry, Mack," she said. "But I really believe you need this. And I don't want you to die."

"Everyone dies, April."

"Not until we have to," she insisted stubbornly. "We don't all have to die in a way that makes no sense."

Except the victims of modern terrorism.

But yeah, he was human. She was right, the lovely lady with the fine mind. He *was* pushing it, maintaining his endless war of containment in a war zone that stretched from one edge to the other of his battle-trained world awareness. Too wide for human comfort, maybe for human survival.

Maybe he did owe it to them.

Maybe he owed it to himself.

So in the end he agreed, and he felt better about it when he had.

But damn it, if he was going to take R and R it would be on his own terms. As with everything Mack Bolan did, it would be without compromise, a challenge and an adventure, time spent in a way that would invigorate the weary body as well as the heavily pressured soul.

He would come back refreshed and ready to rejoin the fight, whole once again. But for a few days—hardly more than a microsecond in the cosmic continuum of time—the fight would briefly cease to exist.

Maybe.

1

The scene looked ordinary enough.

But something about it put Mack Bolan's combat sense on standby alert.

The vehicle was a big late-model Buick sedan with yellow-and-blue California plates. Its right-side wheels were down in the barrow pit along the road, and the left side hugged the shoulder at a too-steep angle. There was no way the stuck Buick was going to make it back onto the pavement under its own power.

Although the highway was a major north-south route, it was isolated enough to remind Bolan that there were still unbelievably vast stretches of open country in the American West. This was the only sort of country where a much called-upon man such as Bolan could get away and breathe freedom for a while. That was what had brought him here.

U.S. Highway 93 runs north from Wickenburg, Arizona. Two hundred miles farther it becomes the southern gateway to Las Vegas, a ten-mile stretch of shopping centers, self-serve gas stations, enough hamburger joints to feed a battalion, with the high-rise pleasure palaces of downtown Las Vegas and the Strip at the farthest end of the city shimmering in the desert heat like a mirage.

From Vegas, Highway 93 heads due north through Nevada, Idaho and Montana to a tiny part-time customs station called Roosville on the Canadian border. Someone had once figured out that there were more people in Bakersfield, California, than there were along this entire 1000-plus-mile length of U.S. highway.

The Buick had picked one of the most isolated stretches of this isolated road to veer into the ditch. The map shows a few towns between Wells, Nevada, and Jackpot, on the Idaho border, but maps exaggerate. Thousand Springs was a ranch headquarters and a long-abandoned general store. San Jacinto and Contact no longer existed. Jackpot was a thriving little community of three hotel-casinos and a trailer village, but the border resort drew nearly all of its clientele from north of the state line.

Since he had left Wells fifteen minutes earlier, the Buick was the only other vehicle Bolan had seen.

This was high-desert country, rolling plains covered with sagebrush, now fragrant after an early-morning rain shower. It was spring, and what sparse grass grew between the sage was just beginning to green up, although way off to the west the peaks of the Independence Mountains were still covered with a mantle of snow. There were a few ranches in this country and nothing else, the ranches owning or holding grazing rights to vast expanses of the desert because it took acres of this scrubland to nourish a steer. In Wells, Bolan had stopped for a cup of coffee and passed the time for a few minutes with a chin-whiskery gent who had lived in the Humboldt River country all his life. "Around here," the old-timer told Bolan, "a cow'd have to have a mouth twenty-five yards wide and be movin' twenty-five miles an hour just to stay alive."

Bolan was almost a mile from the Buick when he topped a rise and spotted it across the vast open prairie. Instinctively he let the Jeep CJ-7 slow a bit while he quick-scanned the situation. The high country still had a brisk chill in the air this time of May, but it was a brilliantly cloudless day after the rain, and the Jeep's top was folded down, giving Bolan an unobstructed view of the land and the great inverted bowl of blue sky atop it.

On the face of it, there was nothing about things here to put Bolan on his guard. The straight monotonous desert road had perhaps given the Buick's driver a slight case of highway hypnosis, made him careless enough to hit the soft shoulder and lose control of the wheel. Probably a couple of breakfast beers had contributed to the mishap. Or it could be just one of those things, an accident that happened to an otherwise careful driver.

Or it could be something else altogether.

In choosing a life of war everlasting, Mack Bolan knew that he was utterly and irrevocably sacrificing his own freedom and security. It was not a war with clearly defined lines and fronts and theaters of operation; it was with him always wherever he went, a smoldering ember that could burst into conflagration at any time. He had already fought in enough unlikely arenas to know that any place he walked was a potential combat zone.

He neither sought nor expected a confrontation on this trip. This was leave time, R and R. But the man was a realist. He had fought too long, strode through too many fiery hellgrounds, single-handedly taken on and crushed too many of the human animals who were dedicated to the oppression of good people everywhere.

As he had tried to convey to his Stony Man colleagues, Bolan knew with moral certainty when he would be finally free of the omnipresent possibility of deadly attack.

It would be the day he died.

He wore jeans, tennis shoes and a nylon windbreaker over a checked flannel shirt. Dark gray sunglasses and a long-billed military-style cap without insignia provided some protection from the thin bright sunshine.

Under the windbreaker, in snap-draw leather, rode a Detonics .45 Associates autoloading pistol. For the first time ever, he had selected a vacation weapon, a piece appropriate for a wary backpacker rather than a blacksuited nightfighter.

The weight of the compact weapon was a reassurance, as well as a constant reminder of the warrior life. Bolan might have preferred to shed the gun and the reminder as well, at least on this vacation trip, but that would neither prove nor accomplish anything. The peril around him was real, and to ever go abroad without a personal side arm was simple foolishness.

The sedan was now a half-mile ahead, as Bolan dropped his speed to a sedate thirty-five miles per hour. Now three doors were open and two men and a woman were standing around the stuck car, even at this distance looking sheepish from their obvious inability to do anything.

Nothing about the men indicated they were anything but early-season tourists up from the Golden Gate State. As Bolan neared, he saw that each man was somewhere in his thirties, dressed casually in slacks and in jackets that were zipped halfway up. The taller one wore a short-brimmed cloth cap, probably with fishing lures hooked into the crown. The shorter one was hatless and had curly hair so blond it was almost white, with a matching mustache.

They were as purely ordinary as possible, but the woman was another story.

She was the same height as the blond man and had a mane of tawny brunette hair that fell in waves. She wore a well-filled halter top, a pair of satin gym shorts and sandals with high cork heels.

Bolan pulled the Jeep over a couple of lengths behind the Buick.

The man in the fishing hat came up and showed him a grin. "Howdy." He glanced back over his shoulder at the Buick and shook his head ruefully. "I guess I took my eyes off the road for a sec. Connie there, she can distract a guy."

"It happens," Bolan said.

"I see you got a winch on your rig," the guy said. "I'd sure appreciate a tow out of that ditch."

"Let me pull around," Bolan told him.

The woman watched as he drove past the Buick and swung around to face it; the winch was mounted above the Jeep's front bumper. The woman looked cold in her brief outfit, and she was a little too made-up for a fishing trip.

Dammit, Bolan told himself, that didn't have to mean anything either. Possibly she was a pro; prostitution was legal in most parts of the state, and she might just be working an extended trick. It was none of his business either way.

Yet he could not shake the feeling that something about the setup was not right. Something he sensed.

As he got out of the Jeep, Bolan glanced again at the two men approaching him. He unobtrusively checked the drape of the front of their jackets for the bulge of a shoulder rig.

Neither wore one.

All right, that was it, Bolan thought. He was a little angry at himself. There was a point where caution could be carried too far; he was acting like an old maid checking under every bed for spooks. For sure, April *had* been right; this vacation was long overdue.

Three tourists had run off the road. Like any other good citizen, Bolan would give them a hand. And then he would be on his way.

"I figured I was looking at a couple of hundred bucks' worth of tow truck for sure," the guy in the hat said. "It'd probably have to come all the way up from Wells, or down from Twin Falls—if you could get hold of one in the first place. Hell, you're the first to come by in fifteen minutes."

Bolan released the cable brake, pulled out the grappling hook, began to pay out steel line toward the Buick. "Glad to help," he said. "Get in and give it some gas when I start up the winch motor. That should do it."

The woman, staring at them from beside the car, had not moved. The light-haired man came around and stood by, like he wanted to help but didn't know quite what was expected of him.

Bolan felt under the bumper for the front axle.

"That ought to do it just fine."

And Bolan knew what was wrong with the setup.

There were no skid marks.

If the guy had lost control at a normal speed of 55 mph and gone shooting off into the sagebrush, maybe there would have been no marks. But if he had managed to wrestle the big sedan to the shoulder, he would have had to leave a sign, tire rubber arcing wildly across the pavement, gravel spewed from tread desperately biting for a hold.

The Buick had not slid into the ditch. It had been parked there.

· Somewhere above Bolan, the scantily dressed woman gasped.

Bolan swung the heavy hook at the end of the steel cable into the tall guy's shin, hard enough to crack bone. The man yowled and fired as Bolan threw his body across the guy's knees. The guy went down backward.

His face was contorted with pain, but he still held the gun. He tried to bring it around, but the drawn Detonics was already in Bolan's swift right hand.

Bolan fired from his knees, the muzzle of the abbreviated weapon less than two feet from the guy's head. The top of his target exploded and a chunky spray of gray and white and red splattered across the roadside gravel.

The woman's gasp had become a scream.

Bolan twisted away as a slug from the surviving guy's gun whined by just inches from his ear and thwacked into the other guy's dead body. The blond man was posed in firing-range stance, his pistol extended stiff-armed in front of him, his left hand supporting his right wrist as he sighted down the short barrel. Although he had succeeded only in plugging a corpse, his posture gave him away as a pro.

Bolan shot him in the calf and slid under the Buick.

The blond guy fired down through the seat and the floorboards, the slug raising a puff of dust six inches wide of Bolan's shoulder. Oil began to leak.

Bolan shot the guy in the other leg.

The heavy .45 slug shattered bone and muscle, and the blond guy sat down in the gravel. Great quantities of blood spurted from the blasted arteries.

"Drop it," Bolan growled from under the car. "You've got less than a minute before you bleed to death."

"Sure," the guy said, with curious detachment, and fired toward Bolan's voice. The bullet pinged into body metal and buried itself somewhere in the dirt, ricocheting off the engine block.

Bolan rolled, came out at the rear end of the car. The woman jumped back away from him, dumbfounded horror in her expression, hysteria in her wide eyes.

The blond gunman lay on his back. A three-foot

circle of blood surrounded his legs, and more pumped from the wound. His face was so twisted with pain it looked as if the muscles were tied in knots.

"Who sent you?" Bolan snapped.

The guy shook his head helplessly. "Finish it... please...."

Bolan rapped out the question a second time. But he had lost the guy. At the last moment something that might have been relief or gratitude cut through the guy's expression of agony, before he went away from his failure and his hurt and his dreadful world of bad men.

Bolan holstered the Detonics. The woman stared at him, took a stumbling backward step, her high heels slipping in the loose gravel along the roadside. She could not tear her wide eyes from him. His jacket was smeared with leaked transmission fluid.

"Connie," Bolan said gently, using the name the tall man had used at the start of this messy and deteriorating scene.

At the sound of her name she began to scream again, this time with the sound of pure panic, more beast than human. She took another step in retreat and fell. She did not try to get up but drew up her knees and buried her face in her arms as the scream subsided into choking sobs.

Bolan let her cry it out while he looked over the two dead men.

Everything about them read professional. Both had carried the same handgun, the new Beretta 92S-2 Compact 9mm automatic—and, as Bolan had observed, *not* in shoulder leather, but in a belt holster worn cunningly at the small of the back. Although less accessible there, the lower spine position was a better place to hide hardware under a decently cut jacket. Additionally, the draw could be concealed until the point where the weapon tracked on target.

The tall man carried a pocket comb and less than $50 in cash. The blond guy had a pack of Marlboros and a book of matches with a blank white cover. Neither had a wallet.

Bolan dragged both bodies behind the Buick and dumped them in the shallow barrow pit. He kicked gravel over the bloodstain on the side of the road.

The tawny-haired girl was sitting in the dirt. She had gotten her crying under control, though her breasts heaved with her hyperventilation. The rouge on her cheeks, streaked with tears, looked like an eroded hillside.

"I'm not going to hurt you," Bolan told her.

She looked up at him. "Listen, I don't know anything about this, I swear to God. Just let me go, and I promise I'll never say anything to anyone. Please."

Bolan reached down his hand. For a long moment she stared at it as if it might bite her. Finally she took it and let him help her up.

"Come on," Bolan said and turned without giving her a chance to argue. He got into the Jeep and the woman slid in on the passenger side. There were no other vehicles on the road in either direction. She sat hunched up against the door as far away from him as she could get, hugging herself with both arms. Bolan dug a denim jacket out of an overnight bag behind his seat. The girl took it wordlessly and wriggled into its oversized depths.

"What were you doing with those men?" Bolan asked quietly.

"They offered me $200," she said. "It was in Reno. All I had to do was ride with them to Twin Falls, and then they'd pay my plane fare back. I needed the money—more than I needed to ask questions."

Bolan offered her a cigarette. He lit it and one for himself. The woman dragged on hers hungrily. Bolan eyed her.

Her look sharpened. "That's the truth, damn it. I'm no whore, if that's what you're thinking. I'm a showgirl—anyway I was in one show, two months ago. I was down on my luck, and I was too broke to care much, as long as they didn't start pawing at me."

"Did they pay you?"

The girl shuddered and nodded yes.

Her story could be checked out, but Bolan believed it. It fit the professionalism of the two hardboys in the ditch. In her skimpy top and short-shorts, the girl was window dressing, misdirection to take Bolan's mind off the snare. Although, of course, she had not succeeded in that. Nothing would have.

So there was no accident to any of this. The ambush was the work of a trained two-man hit team—and according to SOP tradecraft, two men were all you were supposed to need.

It was Mack Bolan's considered opinion, born of his own experience, that their target was no more random than the rest of it.

They knew who they were supposed to hit. They knew that "John Phoenix" would be passing this way.

Bolan cranked the Jeep's ignition.

"Where are we going?" the woman groaned.

"Somewhere safe."

She tried a half-smile. But Bolan's mind was elsewhere, turning over questions and possibilities.

A security leak somewhere.... Were these men free-lancing? Was there now a terrorist price on Bolan? During the Mafia war, the ruling *commissióne* had offered a cool $250,000 for Mack the Bastard's head.

Bolan spun the Jeep around, spitting gravel, and drove north on the empty highway. The woman beside him stared thoughtfully now, as if it had just dawned on her that he was not like the other two. When, a little later, Bolan got out another cigarette for her, she took it from him and lit it, ducking low behind the windshield.

Bolan, also known as John Phoenix, scourge of terrorists, was doing some brooding of his own. And he was coming to a very definite conclusion.

This was one hell of a way to start a vacation.

2

The phone booth was on the edge of the apron of a service station, in the shadow of the only traffic light in Ketchum, Idaho. Bolan was in high-mountain country now. Off to the east he could see Hyndman Peak, its snow-plastered summit rising over 12,000 feet above sea level. In the opposite direction was the jagged ridge of the aptly named Sawtooth Range. A mile or so up the road from the intersection was the world-famous Sun Valley resort.

Bolan unscrewed the mouthpiece of the telephone's handset and replaced it with an identical-looking mouthpiece he took from the pocket of his nylon windbreaker. He dialed "O," then a series of digits that exceeded a standard telephone number. There was a moment of silence, followed by an electronic noise that indicated the safed-and-scrambled connection had been made. A deep voice said, "Go ahead, Mack."

The voice belonged to Aaron "The Bear" Kurtzman, a big rumpled-looking man whose domain was the vast computerized communications and data-system-room at the Stony Man Farm base. Kurtzman rarely left the headquarters, but with electronic links to the computers of the National Security Council, the CIA, and the FBI, as well as those of the Intelligence services of every major friendly nation around the globe, he could do all the traveling he needed from the comfort of his keyboard terminal in the War Room.

"Brief me, Aaron."

"Hal has been in touch with the office of the attorney general of Nevada in Carson City. They've taken over the investigation—except there will not be one. They understand this is a matter of national security."

"Good work." Less than four hours had passed since the attempted bushwack in the Nevada desert had shattered the too-brief tranquillity of Bolan's trip. He had spent a half-hour of that time in the mobile home that served as combination billet and office for the Elko County deputy sheriff assigned to the little gambling oasis of Jackpot. The deputy was a competent-looking guy who listened politely to Bolan, then checked his driver's license with the NSC-cleared special ID. With a slight bit of skepticism he made the phone call that this stranger had requested, listened, nodded twice and handed the phone to Bolan. He watched with respect as Bolan briefly reported what had happened. When Bolan hung up, the deputy said, "I'll take care of this end, sir." Bolan thanked him, shook his hand and went out.

The woman named Connie was waiting for him near the Jeep. She had washed the ruined makeup off her face, and under it was a good-looking woman, with none of the brittleness Bolan had first observed in her.

"I owe you," she said softly. She put her hand on Bolan's arm, and he could feel its tender nature through his jacket.

"You had a bad break," he said. "Forget it happened."

She gazed at him. "In what I do...where I live and all...well, I meet a lot of pretty crummy guys. Those two that you...those two were the worst. But then a guy doesn't need a gun to hurt a girl, if you know what I mean." There was color high up on her cheeks. "I don't know who you are, but I do know you're one of the good guys. That's enough for me." She looked away. "I guess it would be best if I forget all this, huh?"

Bolan nodded.

She brightened a little. "Maybe it's a sign. You know, maybe you gotta hit bottom before you get going on a roll toward the top."

"Good luck, Connie." Bolan started the Jeep's engine.

"Sure," she said softly. "Same to you, Mister Good Guy."

Bolan had felt her eyes on him as he pulled out past Cactus Pete's Casino and back onto Highway 93, pointing the Jeep north.

All of that passed through his mind as he stood now in the phone booth beneath Ketchum's sole traffic light. "What about the woman?" he asked Kurtzman.

"She was your proverbial innocent bystander, like you figured. She's been questioned and sent home."

A young man and a girl went by the phone booth,

holding hands. The woman was laughing. "Those two gunmen?" Bolan asked.

Static and scrambler clicks welled up to fill a momentary pause. Then April's voice said, "Nothing yet, Mack. We've cross-queried the likely data banks and come up with a blank. The guns were clean, too, legitimately purchased by private citizens and later reported stolen by person or persons unknown. The Buick was rented in Tahoe on the California side with a credit card—an excellent counterfeit. Sorry, Mack, that's all for now. We're still working on it."

Bolan got a cigarette lit and cracked open the door of the phone booth to let smoke drift out. So far the conversation had brought up more questions than it answered.

"What now, Mack?"

"Now," Bolan said lightly, "I'm going to take a river trip, as I planned. You're not forgetting whose idea this is, are you?"

"Mack...."

She was concerned, sure. The woman had dedicated her life to supporting his campaigns, and she had accepted the decision that put his life on the line for the rest of his days. Yet she was his lover, and she could never completely banish worry from her mind.

"Based on what we've got so far," Bolan pointed out, "there's no compelling reason for me to change my plans."

"At least make contact when you get—"

"Let's see now," Bolan interrupted, teasing her. "Who said a couple of days ago, 'The world will manage to make a few revolutions without Mack Bolan around to see that it doesn't wobble'?''

"Okay," April said wearily. She sighed. "Have a good one. Think of me." Then, in a rush, "I love you, Mack."

"Give that Salmon River hell, Mack," said Kurtzman. "Let it know it's been licked." A series of beeps and scratches signaled the breaking of the scrambled connection.

The Jeep was parked across the street, in front of a gallery selling Western art. A woman stood next to it, staring at a bronze of a cavalry troop in the gallery window. She turned as Bolan came up. She was tall and lithe and had straight coal-black hair and a delicately featured olive-skinned face. She wore a small orange daypack.

"Are you heading north?" she asked. "I could use a lift to Stanley."

Bolan hesitated. He would enjoy the company—but the memory of the Nevada ambush was too fresh in his mind. Bolan was a lodestone for violence. It was neither fair nor responsible to wittingly allow any innocent person to enter his dangerous sphere.

The little things he was forced to eschew—like the companionship of an attractive stranger for one hour out of a lifetime—sometimes caused the greatest pangs in the man's heart.

"You're not afraid of Indians, are you?" the dark-haired girl asked lightly. "I haven't scalped a white man in a week."

Bolan grinned. "Sorry. I . . . ."

"That's okay," the girl said. "You know what

John Wayne says in *She Wore a Yellow Ribbon*:
'Don't apologize. It's a sign of weakness.' '' She gave
him a faint sardonic smile and turned back to the
gallery window.

When he pulled out of town, she was framed in the
rearview mirror, standing beneath the traffic light
with her thumb out. Bolan felt bad about that.

Aaron Kurtzman leaned across the control console
and flipped a toggle to break the scrambled phone
connection. In a wall rack two reel-to-reel tape
recorders ganged to the line automatically clacked to
a stop. Kurtzman turned his swivel chair to face
April, sitting alone at the big oak conference table
that dominated the windowless room. He dug his
pipe out of the pocket of his lab coat and tamped
dark tobacco into its bowl, then patted absently at his
other pockets for matches.

"So far, looking for facts has drawn a blank," he
said. "Let's try hunches."

April tossed a book of matches to Aaron, who
caught it clumsily. "A contract?" she suggested.
"Someone's put paper on him?"

"Anything's possible in this world." Kurtzman
swung back to his terminal. His fingers played over
the keyboard and words began to stream across the
display screen.

"Questions," he said, typing them as he formu-
lated them aloud. "One, who were those men? Two,
how did they identify Mack? Three, how did they
pinpoint his whereabouts? Four, assuming they were
professionals, whom did they work for? Five, were

they self-contained or part of a larger assault force? And six, if the latter, what are the continuing short-term ramifications?"

April gave him a thoughtful look. "There could be others on Mack's tail right now."

"Correct."

"All right," April said briskly. "Let's try to find some answers."

"Already on it." New lines of video-generated text were appearing before him.

"Meanwhile, what do we do to secure Mack?"

Kurtzman stopped typing. He took time to relight his pipe. "I think we do nothing, April," he said cautiously. "We know we can't baby-sit the guy—he's never stood for it. In lieu of Intelligence to the contrary, we must assume he is in the clear for now." The match burned his fingertips, and he shook it out absently. "April, there isn't a minute in any hour of any of Mack Bolan's days when he isn't walking the knife-edge between living and dying. He's accepted that, and we have to do the same."

"We could call him in."

"No, we could not," Kurtzman said. "No one calls Mack Bolan in, not even you. And anyway, trouble he can handle, right?"

The Bear flashed her a reassuring smile and turned back to his data scan, but his last words echoed in April's mind. *Trouble he can handle, right?*

So Mack would get his R and R and no doubt come back refreshed and renewed and in one piece. It made more sense to worry about him hitting his head on a river rock than being attacked in the middle of the Idaho Primitive Area.

When there was trouble he would handle it—in the way he always had.

For Mack Bolan, trouble was always as near as the next river bend.

And serious was the only way it came.

3

Mack Bolan had been a superior athlete from the earliest days of his youth. Speed, agility and coordination came naturally to him, and from his burly steelworker father he inherited a sturdy physique. He enjoyed making demands upon his body, and staying in shape became as much a habit as eating.

But competitive sports never held much attraction for the young Bolan. The only meaningful competition was against oneself. Perhaps competition was not the right word; it was more that you pushed yourself—to the limits of endurance, capacity and capability, and in coming back from those limits learned a lesson more valuable than that gained from besting another person.

In his lifetime Bolan had tried surfing, hang gliding, rock and ice climbing, and spelunking, or deep cave exploring. Sure, there was an element of risk, but more important was the challenge of pitting himself against nature in all her wildest forms—and overcoming, prevailing, surviving.

What he learned in the wilderness of nature later served him well in the jungles of man.

Bolan had had his first white-water experience at nine, in a little stream not far from his Pittsfield,

Massachusetts home. The normally placid creek was swollen by an unusually rainy spring, and Bolan had bummed an inner tube from a service station and negotiated the roiling water in it. He was dumped out twice and carried nearly a half-mile farther than he had reckoned on.

But he made it in one piece.

He was late for supper, and when his mother asked why, he told her the truth. The good Elsa gave him a stormy look and turned it on his father. The look said: "You handle him, Sam." His father arose from the table and sternly ordered his son out back.

Once there the older Bolan asked, "Do you think that was a foolish thing to do, riding that river?"

Bolan gave the question careful consideration. "Not foolish," he said slowly. "I guess I did bite off more than I'd figured on." Then he brightened. "But I managed to chew it."

His father nodded solemnly. "You remember that lesson," he said, "and we'll forget the rest."

"Thanks, dad."

"It wouldn't hurt if you had a long expression on your face when we go back in," Sam Bolan said, though his own eyes were twinkling. "It never hurts to let a woman think she got what she was after."

By his twelfth year Bolan had progressed from inner tubes through rafts to canoes, and his dad joined in, the two taking camping trips into the Berkshires, the Green Mountains of Vermont, the Adirondacks in upstate New York. The recollections of those days in the forest, no one around but the two of them, and the swift-running mountain streams they defied and subdued together, were some of the most vivid memories of his late father that Bolan carried.

When he was fourteen, Bolan discovered kayaks and knew that no craft but the sleek one-man boat would ever satisfy him again.

In a kayak a man could control his destiny on the river as in no other craft. Seated in the open port, legs extended straight toward the bow, a waterproof spray skirt covering the opening, Bolan became an extension of the boat. Combining the use of the double-bladed paddle with his own balance and coordination, he could make the boat react instantly. A kayak was so responsive and sensitive that a single paddle-stroke could turn it 180 degrees.

The first time his kayak turned turtle and Bolan found himself hanging upside down in the water, he quickly pulled the spray skirt free, pushed himself clear and came up, holding on to boat and paddle. He then spent a half-hour sitting on the bank, staring at the boat, considering its shape, hefting the paddle and turning it this way and that, pondering. Then he relaunched, cruised to a flat smooth place in the river and flipped again—this time deliberately.

He hung there, every move carefully calculated. He braced the paddle in position, took a long sweeping stroke and snapped his hips in the direction of the force exerted, his head breaking water last. He halfway made it—before tumbling upside down again. But at least he managed to grab a breath of air.

It took him five tries. After the fifth he was gasping from oxygen deprivation and exertion, and trembling from the water's cold and the ache of his muscles.

But he was upright again.

The young Bolan believed he had invented a new kayak technique. So at first he was deflated when an older kayaker, who had watched his practice, told him that the Eskimo roll was the basic alternative to a "wet exit." But when the older guy learned that the young man had taught himself the maneuver—and in less than ten minutes—Bolan saw the respect in his expression and felt a little better.

On leave during his years in the army, before his personal wars had been declared, Bolan refined and honed his kayaking skills on rivers all over the U.S. and Europe. So it was not unexpected that on this leave he would return to that ultimate confrontation: man vs. raging white-water rapids.

He had just the spot picked out, too. Though he had never actually run this course, he had heard and read enough to know that if anything would get the kinks out, it was this.

They called it the River of No Return.

It had earned its name.

Bolan piloted the Jeep CJ-7 over the 8700-foot Galena Summit, and as the switchbacks on the north side that descended into the Sawtooth Valley began to straighten, he got his first glimpse of the Salmon River.

Even here, only a few miles below the high-mountain lakes and melting snowfields that formed the river's headwaters, the flow was, yeah, impressive. Before committing to the trip, Bolan had done some checking. He had learned the snowfall during the previous months had been slightly above average, and that factor, combined with an early spring thaw that lasted a good two weeks, followed by two more of rain, had swollen the tributaries of the vast Salmon River system to the limits of their banks. Now, in mid-May, the river, not yet more than ten feet wide as it took its first step toward the Snake River, and then the Columbia, and finally the Pacific Ocean, was thick and tumbling and angry, daring someone to take it on.

Okay, Brother River, Bolan thought. I'll take that dare.

For the next 170 miles, Highway 93 followed the stream, clinging to the roadbed gouged out of the side of the steep-walled canyon. This had been mining country once. Beginning in the 1870s, the hills had swarmed with newly arrived prospectors bitten hard by the gold bug. Now, Bolan drove past roadside signs memorializing those played-out mines and the ghost towns left behind along with them: the Nip-n-Tuck, the Yankee Fork, the Charles Dickens, the Golden Sunbeam.

There was something deeply reassuring about those names and the history they represented. Bolan had deliberately chosen to fly only as far as Salt Lake City, where he had rented the Jeep. He had a hunch that driving the last five hundred miles might serve as a way of putting his own life in perspective. For too long he had been hurtling around the world fighting for his country—and in the process had perhaps lost firsthand touch with that country. Now he had a chance to see how America was doing for itself.

To Mack Bolan's eye, it was doing fine.

In the small Idaho towns along the route—Stanley, Challis, Salmon—people with their roots in the rugged West looked hale and fit after the rigors of winter. North of Challis, where the canyon opened into a wide bottomland swale, ranchers were rounding up their herds, counting the new calves that would someday be reincarnated as prime beef on America's dinner plates.

Fences were being mended, irrigation gates opened and water balanced, kitchen gardens planted. Bolan stopped and watched two men—they looked to be father and son—working cows from horseback. The older man was cutting off calves from their mothers.

The big blue-roan quarter horse the man was riding moved quick and graceful as a dancer, slicing a calf from the herd, darting to head off the dull-faced critter when it got contrary. As the calf was clear, the man tossed a rope under its front hooves and took a few turns around his saddle horn, while his son hind-legged the animal and did the same.

When the two men dismounted, their horses did not move except to backstep, if necessary, to keep tension on the trussed calf. The horses' cow-sense was the result of rigorous training and breeding.

The son fetched an iron from where it rested in a bed of glowing red hardwood embers, held it against the calf's flank for a few seconds. When he pulled it clear, the fresh brand was sooty black against the animal's singed hide. A few moments later the ropes were off and being coiled, and the bewildered animal was trotting unsteadily back to the herd.

Some things did not change, Bolan knew. Men in the West had been working cattle the same way for well over a century, fighting hard winters and dry summers and coyotes, four- and two-legged both, to keep butchers' display cases full of neatly dressed cuts of meat, and fast-food hamburgers churning out by the billions. And hard as it was to eke a decent living from this land by growing beef, the cowman would have no other life.

Here was a continuity, an unbroken line to the past and a commemoration of all the muscle and sweat and determination that had gone into building the country's foundation. This was what made it all worthwhile.

This was what Mack Bolan fought to preserve. Seeing it before him this way, he knew again that the fight was worth it.

Bolan spent the night in a motel in the town of Salmon, checking in with the John Doe-type anonymity granted by his officially rigged ID.

He ate a steak and afterward did something that he had not done in longer than he could remember, certainly since before the dark days of the Mafia war: he went into a tavern and drank a few beers. It felt good being in the company of men and women again, even as a stranger. The man on the next barstool, a bluff redheaded young guy with forearms like shillelaghs and a ready open smile, wanted to talk about the prospects of the Seattle Mariners that season. Bolan

barely had time for the sports pages recently, but he
listened, nodded when appropriate, and bought the
guy a beer, enjoying the companionship of the conversation.

He was in North Fork, another twenty miles downriver, early the next morning. From here Highway 93
continued north, while the river took an abrupt jog
left, westward. A paved secondary road followed the
river for seventeen miles, then turned to gravel for
another thirty. River-runners generally put in at
its end, because only wilderness embraced the next
seventy-five miles of boiling white water. The put-out
was at another tongue of gravel road, and twenty-
five miles past it, civilization reasserted itself in the
form of the town of Riggins.

Because the roadless stretch of the River of No
Return was extremely popular with rafters, canoeists,
and kayakers alike, the U.S. Forest Service held a
competitive drawing for access permits during the
height of the season. But in May, when Bolan came
to the river country, no permit was required—because few were gutsy enough to try the big water of
spring runoff.

"Gutsy" was not exactly the word the fellow in the
North Fork store used when Bolan came into his
establishment to outfit for the trip.

"You're crazy, friend," he commented genially.
The place was comfortably old-fashioned, a general
store in the traditional manner. On one side was a
café, on the other everything from hunting and fishing gear to clothing, hardware and groceries. Twin
islands of gas pumps were out front.

"That's no way to talk to a paying customer."
Bolan grinned.

"Not a customer of mine, not if you're looking to
rig for a kayaking trip. What kind of deal is it for me
if all of the gear I rent you ends up smashed against
the rocks at the bottom of a suckhole?"

"If I thought that would happen," Bolan said
evenly, "I wouldn't be here."

The store manager's eyes narrowed as he gave
Bolan a closer look. "So you think you know what
you're doing, eh?"

"That's right."

The manager fished a tin of chewing tobacco from
the pocket of his checked wool shirt and stuck a
pinch between his gum and lip, mostly to be doing
something with his hands while he gave this matter
some thought.

"In 1911," he said slowly, "a man named John
Painter posted a mining claim almost one hundred
miles downriver from here. He needed machinery
brought in, so he hired old Harry Guleke, the greatest boatman on Salmon River, then or ever. Everyone said even Cap Guleke would never make it."

The manager spit into a coffee can on the counter.
"There was ninety thousand pounds of mining gear,
and Cap built nine barges to haul it, all wood, nearly
forty feet long and each one of them near as hard to
handle as a strong-minded woman. That was before
some of the falls had been dynamited, too, so what
Cap meant to do was damned near impossible, by
any sane man's lights." He spit again. "You know
what happened?"

"He made it," Bolan said.

"That's right."

"Then you'll rent me some gear." Bolan smiled.

"Well, hell," the manager said resignedly. "This is the West. In these parts a man can do what he pleases—even if he is crazy as a ground squirrel."

Bolan chose a Precision Mirage kayak made of a virtually indestructible polymer plastic. The Mirage was an all-purpose fusiform design with a low deck and well- rounded gunwales, basically a slalom kayak more than a downriver racer, which meant greater stability and easier Eskimo rolls. But the main factor in Bolan's decision was the Mirage's maneuverability and its incredible responsiveness to every nuance of the boater's stroke and movement.

In the most treacherous of rapids, the Mirage would glide smooth as thought.

Bolan selected a double-blade laminated hardwood paddle, with square-tipped concave blades on a right-twist handle for maximum effectiveness during turns and minimum slip during flat-water strokes. For a spare he took a two-piece model that joined by means of a light metal ferrule and held in place with a set-screw. The metal sleeve was a potential weak point and the paddle was heavier, but the breakdown feature allowed it to be stowed inside the Mirage's hull—and it would for sure come in handy if the laminated paddle were broken or lost. Additional equipment included a black neoprene spray skirt with an adjustable elastic draw-cord that fit around the coaming, which was the out-turned lip that ran around the perimeter of the cockpit.

Bolan spent some time going over the wet suits, the one piece of gear absolutely essential to survival. At this time of year the water would be close to freezing, and at that temperature an unprotected person lasts no more than a few minutes before hypothermia takes lethal effect. He finally settled on a Wilderness Seasuit long-sleeve jacket and a matching Farmer John-style coverall with built-in knee pads for cushioning during bracing against the inside of the craft. He also selected a holstered knife. A pair of the new Tabata Wet Shoes completed the outfit; these were a combination of a wet-suit boot and a thick ribbed rubber sole for traction and durability.

The entire skintight outfit was strikingly similar to Bolan's blacksuit, the midnight bodycover that was his standard uniform for infiltration and blitzing.

For most boaters the Main Fork Salmon run was at least three days long. Bolan planned to take it with a single overnight, and he geared up accordingly with an eye to light traveling. A goose-down sleeping bag, a three-quarter-length ground pad, and an assortment of lightweight cold food and high-energy snacks went into two waterproof Bills Bags; the heavy-duty PVC-coated Dacron sacks could be stowed in the fore and aft compartments of the closed kayak to do double duty as flotation aids. The Detonics merited a small Tuck Sack of its own. A small first-aid kit, a Cooper kayaking helmet, and a Type III personal flotation device comprised the safety equipment.

By ten that morning Bolan was back on the road,

heading the Jeep down into the valley of the River of
No Return.

AT FIRST there was no hint of the hellroaring cascade
it would become. For five miles west of North Fork,
the stream meandered through a shallow cut dotted
with clusters of range cattle grazing the rich bottomland's lush grassy carpet. To Bolan's right the
slope running up to the ridgeline was covered with
sagebrush and cheat grass, but the opposite side,
across the river, was forested with thick stands of
Douglas fir. Bolan could smell their aroma, fragrant
with pitch.

Farther on, a bright orange wind sock was planted
on a hump above the roadway, pointing stiffly west.
Just past was the ranger station at Indianola, a
cluster of Forest-Service-green buildings to the right
of the road and a helitack base on the left. When the
regular river season opened, the grassy landing zone
would be home to a little two-seater bubblefront
chopper stationed there for emergency rescue assign-
ments and fire reconnaissance.

A few miles after that, Salmon River began to
reveal its true nature.

Where Pine Creek joined the Salmon, the gravel
road crossed the main stream on a steel-and-concrete
flat-span bridge. Bolan parked the Jeep on the far
side and walked back out to the center. From there he
could check out Pine Creek Rapids, the first major
white water on this part of the Salmon, nicknamed
the ''River of No Return'' because travel upstream
was thought impossible.

Bolan intended to prove the river's nickname a lie.

He would, yeah, return.

Huge granite boulders were strewed across the river coursing below him, some with their craggy tops above water, others lurking below the surface. Water cascaded around and among and over them, making a rushing crescendo roar that never peaked. The shape and position of the rocks dictated the course and form of any rapids, and in this white water the boulders had conspired to form a menacing obstacle to safe passage. Bolan made out three primary channels, but each came with a warning.

The one on the far left took the intrepid adventurer through a series of standing waves at least four feet high, haystack whitecaps that faced upriver and chewed into the bow of any boat that entered them. The middle channel passed between two towering rock sentinels—and then headed directly for a third, requiring a near-ninety-degree turn if the boat was to avoid it and at the same time keep its bow pointed downriver. The right channel passed between a rock and a suckhole, the latter at least three feet deep. Caused by the undercurrent of the river passing over a large underwater rock, these holes possessed hydrodynamically complex forces powerful enough to draw even a life-jacketed man down into them, holding the victim until he had the sense to dive deep enough to catch the downstream current. Or until he drowned.

And Pine Creek Rapids was just a sneak preview.

Lurking downriver were its relatives, each one uniquely treacherous, a supreme challenge to the most expert boatman. The river would have seventy-five miles' worth of chances to chew up Bolan and spit out the pieces.

Unless it decided to swallow him whole.

Bolan shot the river a broad grin before hurrying back to the Jeep.

He could hardly wait to let it take its best shot.

4

The sign above the log building read Gold Bar Creek Café and General Store, and the one on the front door said Closed, but there was a car parked around the side of the structure, and a woman halfway up a stepladder was cleaning one of the big front windows. The car was a Nash Rambler that must have been twenty-five years old; the woman was thin and sharp-featured with hair the color and texture of barbed wire. She wore a button-front sweater over a housedress and looked somewhere in her fifties.

With a stern expression she watched Bolan get out of the Jeep, as if she were about to challenge his right to do so. But then she came down the ladder and draped her washrag over a rung. She stood arms akimbo and gave him a frank once-over.

"You ain't with them others," she announced, as if she had come to an important decision in Bolan's favor.

"I didn't see any others," Bolan said. "I was beginning to think there wasn't anyone around here this time of the year."

"There ain't, except a few river folk." The woman spit into the dust in front of Bolan's tennis shoes. "Normally," she added.

A warning prickled his senses. "But you say some others passed this way?"

"Have you had lunch, young man?" the woman said. This was her territory, and she was in charge. If she were going to tell him anything, Bolan would have to wait patiently until she was ready.

He gestured at the Closed sign. He guessed she'd have a better time if she had to talk him into it.

"What are you going to pay attention to, me or that darned-fool sign?" the woman demanded. "I don't open up officiallike for another month, but I always come up early, soon as the snow's cleared off the road. Winters I stay with my son and his wife in Boise, and after three months of his fancy city airs and her bellyachin', I can't wait to get back up here by myself. 'Course, a body needs company once in a while, and you look a sight nicer than them others."

"What didn't you like about them?" Bolan tried politely.

"You come on in now," the woman ordered. "I got everything on my menu from T-bone steaks to calves' brains and eggs. But the only thing in the refrigerator is hamburgers. That's a joke, young man."

"Hamburgers would be fine, Mrs....?"

"Poten. Jane C. Poten. And it's 'Miss.' I never did hold with any man enough to want to get all tied up with him."

"I'm John, Miss Poten."

"Just John, eh?" Miss Poten furrowed her brow. "Well, that's enough for me."

The hamburgers were thick and juicy and hand-formed from beef that Miss Poten had ground herself. Suddenly Mack Bolan was enormously hungry. The clear mountain air sharpened his appetite, and he ate two hamburgers and had to work hard to keep Miss Poten from forcing a third on him. When he was finished, she poured coffee, sat down to frame her cup with her bony elbows and said, "Now then, John, my man: what is your business in Salmon River country at this outlandish time of spring?"

He told her, and she guffawed. "In this big water?"

Bolan smiled. "I don't have time to wait for it to go down."

Miss Poten frowned at his directness. "Young man, it's not for me to say you're pure loco. Maybe reckless is more like it. Folk have died in that white water."

"Have you lived on Salmon River long?" Bolan asked.

"Near all my life."

"It must be a bit difficult, living all the way up here by yourself. Dangerous, too. If you got sick or hurt...."

"I'd doctor myself like I always have. Anyway, I'm too bony to give the devil a good meal. And like the man says, if it ain't worth working for, it ain't worth having."

"I guess that's how I see it." Bolan grinned. He started to reach for the cigarette pack in his shirt pocket, then hesitated.

"Go ahead and smoke, young man," Miss Poten

snapped. "I give up them tobacco sticks two years ago, but I don't care what you do or don't do."

Bolan lit his cigarette. "I guess you were surprised to see so many strangers on the river this time of year, then," he suggested casually. Deeply ingrained military habits forced him to probe, soft or hard, whenever his survival senses were tickled by clues that would not go away. Right now the probe was as soft as they come. But his combat alertness was bright and firm, insistent on answers. For the clues refused to die in his mind, slight though they were.

"Well now, there was plenty in the old days," Miss Poten declared, avoiding the issue until it was time to get around to it. "Miners and prospectors crawling all over these mountains searching for their fortunes. I never held with it myself. Hard work and the brains God gave you keep you on the path to prosperity, I say. My but that cigarette smells fine."

Miss Poten poured more coffee. "Now the mines and the placers are all played out, and mostly the only reason people come into the country is hunting, fishing and boating. But hunting season is in the fall, the water's too muddy and roily for fishing, and too mean and rough for boats—unless you've got more grit than horse sense." She shot Bolan a pointed look, and he put on a properly solemn expression for her.

"Most of the lodges and pack camps and boat out-fitters won't be opened up for another two, three weeks. 'Bout the only place doing business is the Kerr place. The Tide Creek Lodge, they call it, on account of a little wash by that name coming down the mountainside there. And they would of been closed up too, if it wasn't for them others.''

"Which others, Miss Poten?"

"John, have you been paying attention?" She looked to Bolan for all the world like a stern schoolmarm. "I mentioned them others soon as I laid eyes on you.''

"Who were they, Miss Poten?"

Instead of answering, the sharp-featured woman rose abruptly and went to the window. She stood there with her back to Bolan. Beyond her he could see nearly a half-mile of river and the high snow-dusted ridge in the distance.

"There's people who come into this country and seem to understand it right off," Miss Poten said without turning. "They know that as far as the wilderness goes you are the outsider, and you don't pollute it with your ways or try to make it over in your own citified image. You live with it, harmonize with it like in a barbershop quartet. You let it change *you*, and you listen to what the country has to tell you, because you might learn something.''

She slowly turned and impaled Bolan with a steely gaze. "Then there is others who come in and are blind as moles. Them are the ones go barreling past in their big shiny pickup trucks, raising up clouds of road dust for the devil of it, and flipping their beer cans and cigarette butts into the bitterbush. Them are the ones 'jacking mulie deer with car headlights, and catching way over their limit of fish just to toss 'em into the willows and leave 'em to rot. Then they go back to the city and brag about what fine, bold woodsmen they are.''

"Who were the men who passed earlier, Miss Poten?'' Bolan asked.

"You answer me a question first, young man. Are you truthin' when you say the only reason you are here is to kayak that hellroaring river? Are you sure it don't have nothing to do with those men?''

"I told you the truth. I don't know who those men are.''

"But you might—sometime. Never you mind,'' Miss Poten went on quickly. "In the West you don't start in on pryin' into other folks' business, so I ain't about to ask what your workaday line is. But I got a sense about people, and it ain't failed me yet. There is blood on your hands, young man.''

Bolan was startled, but maintained his poise.

"Which maybe don't mean so much,'' Miss Poten went on. "We've had a war. Many men have killed. Whoever's blood it was, deserved to shed it. You are a good man, John, that's what I think.''

Bolan looked at her impassively, yet there was gratitude in his eyes.

"But there's violence in you all the same.'' Finally she came back to the table and sat down again. "So's I guess I better tell you what I know—and what I feel as well, seein' as how it's just as reliable. I don't want you going off half-cocked and hell-for-leather.''

She took a sip of coffee. "Last afternoon, maybe three hours this side of sundown, I heard 'em coming. Sounds travel in this canyon. I went out for a look. They was in the big yellow school bus that Vern

Travers uses to bring folk down to Corn Creek for the raft trips he runs, but he don't start 'til next month, so I reckoned he rented it out. Anyway, they eyeball me and the bus stops and the driver asks how far to the boat ramp at Corn, so's I had a chance to get a look at 'em, settin' there in the bus.

"They was all men, a couple dozen or more, dressed up in denims and huntin' caps and hikin' boots and so forth, like a man wears for the woods, nothin' wrong—and *that* was what was wrong. They looked like they just stepped out of a L.L. Bean catalog, outfitted up and ready to go. I say to myself, 'Miss Jane, here is a mess of folks tryin' to look like somethin' they ain't.' ''

"They said they were going to Tide Creek Lodge?'' Bolan asked.

"Rein up, young man,'' Miss Poten admonished. "You'll have me gettin' ahead of myself. That's what I figured, 'cause there wasn't any other place. Corn is where the lodge guests leave their vehicles, too. The Kerrs got a jet boat they use to bring 'em downriver the last five miles.

"Then, maybe an hour later, Casey and Ella Kerr come rattlin' up in their old beater, and they stop to jaw like they always do. Turns out these characters in the bus had called just that mornin' and arranged to come right on in. Somehow they knew the Kerrs were the only river folk who stayed in all year round, and that the lodge would be empty of payin' customers this time of year. And while it wouldn't be mannerly to discuss other folks' money matters, I can tell you that these city people offered a bushel, and the Kerrs needed it bad as sin.

"But they was going to turn 'em down anyway. You see, Case's gall bladder's been going back on him, and he was all set to get flown up to the hospital in Missoula, where the sawbones was going to cut the little sucker out of him for good and all. It'd taken most of the winter for Ella to talk Case into having the operation, and she was afraid to postpone it. But Johnny piped up and told them to go ahead, that he could handle the place and the guests, too."

"Johnny?"

"Johnny Kerr." Miss Poten's expression softened at the name. "Case and Ella's pup. Only halfway to being a man, but tough enough to fight mountain lions bare-handed. Johnny grew up in this country and spent all his days in the woods or on the water. He's a river-rat and a hellcat, that boy. Crazier maybe than you—but, of course, you're old enough to know better."

"I guess I am," Bolan agreed. There was something he liked very much about this woman. She had known him for maybe a half hour, but it seemed as if they had been close much longer. And behind her scolding, Bolan detected true concern. And goodness and strength.

"Do you have a telephone, Miss Poten?"

"Never had need for one, young man. If I'm talkin' to a body, I want to see his face."

Bolan would take that as an omen. Vacation this would be, and he would pursue it as relentlessly as anything else he took on. No contact with April and Aaron unless he was really pushed.

"You make a fine hamburger, Miss Poten. What do I owe you?"

"Young man!" she snapped, and again Bolan had the feeling he had been caught cutting up in grade school. "Don't you know when you've been guested?"

"Thank you."

"You spent a half hour listenin' to me jaw on. I guess that's thanks and pay enough."

He shook hands with the woman, and she held his in both of hers and did not let go.

"You take care of yourself," she said softly. "I'd wish you luck, but you strike me as the sort of fellow who makes his own luck."

"Everyone needs luck, Miss Poten."

"Including you," she said, stern again, "if you insist on going down that man-eating river."

But as he started out the door she spoke once more, her tone quiet again, as if she were thinking out loud for Bolan's benefit.

"John, you know I told you there was two kinds come into this country?"

"Yes."

"Them men, they were the second kind. They were afraid of the wilderness. And because of that they're dangerous. They'll strike out at it, thinkin' that by gettin' in the first licks they'll be all right. Only there's one thing they don't know."

Bolan waited.

"The wild country's got ways of gettin' back at

folks like that. Sometimes them ways are mean, and not always pretty.''

Bolan appreciated her concern, admired her wisdom. He knew well enough that she was damned right.

He knew because he himself had the nature of the wilderness in him.

He resembled the extremes of the untamed regions when he was called to do so, and his methods, of necessity, were always direct, often furious, and not always pretty.

Within an hour, the ways of the wild country and the ways of The Executioner would come together.

5

Gauge markings on the concrete boat ramp indicated the river water's level; a sign on the beach above it interpreted that figure. The sign had three columns, and Bolan sought the figure 6½ feet in the one on the left and read across.

Under River Flow he read 23,251 cfs.

Under Degree of Danger he read High to Extreme.

A few yards away, the River of No Return careered past in a constant rumble. Bolan eyed it with respect and anticipation.

There was an A-frame ranger station here at the Corn Creek Boat Access, but it would not be staffed until mid-June when the permit system took effect. Near the boat ramp was a floating wooden pier. The jet boat, which transported guests across and upriver the mile or so to the Salmon River Lodge, docked here. Beyond the A-frame was a campground, and above it a parking area defined by a post-and-pole fence. The yellow school bus that Miss Poten had described was the only vehicle there.

Bolan unloaded the Jeep at the top of the concrete ramp, then parked and secured it next to the bus. He descended to the boat ramp with the kayak held above his head.

Chill brisk air washed over him as he put the kayak down, then stripped to the skin and pulled on the wet suit. The waterproof Bills Bags were already packed and it took only a few minutes to stow them fore and aft of the kayak, along with the two halves of the spare paddle. A lightweight nylon belt went around the waist of the wet suit.

On the left hip Bolan strapped a sheathed buck knife, and a pocket-sized waterproof Tuff Sack containing cigarettes and two disposable lighters. From the belt's opposite side hung a second sack for the Detonics and a spare clip.

Bolan stepped into the detached neoprene spray skirt and pulled it up over the belt so it girded his lower chest. Next he slipped on the PFD and fastened the helmet's strap under his chin.

There was a back eddy, at the upstream end of the boat ramp, where the water swirled out of the main current toward shore and then in the opposite direction, a gentle half-whirlpool. Bolan set the light kayak in there, laid the paddle across the back of the coaming with one blade resting on the concrete for stabilization, and eased himself into the cockpit, stretching his feet straight out to the pegs, flexing his knees against the control bracings. He snapped the spray skirt around the coaming's lip.

With the boat facing upstream, Bolan gave a hard right-side forward stroke, and the nose was caught by the heady current, turning the boat in a quick sweep downstream into the channel. Paddle held overhead like a barbell, Bolan tilted it to dig in the downstream blade as he leaned in the same direction in a high brace, a maneuver in which the paddle served as a lever against the fulcrum of the water's normal resistance.

Within seconds Corn Creek access was out of sight behind the bend and Mack Bolan was racing downriver.

The water was high and very fast, but between the rapids there were stretches where it ran relatively smoothly. Later in the summer, when the water went down, these places would be placid as lakes, but in this flow no part of the river gave the boater more than time enough to catch his breath and get his bearings.

As soon as he had the feel of the Mirage, Bolan drew his paddle, leaned far right, and let himself flip upside down. Ice-cold water washed inside the wet suit, but Bolan hardly noticed it. There was too much else to occupy the man's senses.

Below the surface turbulence the water was more clear. A few feet under his helmeted head the rocky river bottom swept by; to his left, hidden underwater and just out of his path, was a granite boulder sharp enough to gut an inflatable raft. Despite the apparent awkwardness of his position, totally upside down and hanging from the kayak, the unguided Mirage plummeting down the raging channel, Bolan felt a heady exhilaration. This subsurface recon was a necessary familiarization with the elements into which he was voluntarily and unhesitatingly plunging.

He leaned forward, set the paddle, then swept it hard around, moving into a strong backward lean as the control hand cleared the hull. He snapped his hips hard and popped upright as easily as a bathtub toy.

Bolan laughed out loud, the sound free and clear and musical on the brilliant sweet spring mountain air.

The body remembered, he thought with vast joy. It remembered those days a lifetime before, on the piney-woods streams in New England, the freedom of the pell-mell downriver scramble, the excitement of melding with the water and becoming fluid. The body remembered and knew itself, now reveled in the power of its skills retained after all these years!

Ahead Bolan could hear the roar of Gunbarrel Rapids.

Here the water shot straight through between the steep banks, falling quickly as it coursed over a rock eddy deep underwater. In fact, the high volume had partially washed the rapid out, but it was the first one in his campaign against this river, and Bolan meant to get through as neatly as possible. He spotted the V-channel where the water funneled in its natural path and corrected his progress so that he came through the apex of it.

The bow of the Mirage shot downward, and two-foot-high standing waves washed over it. Bolan's paddle took shallow bites at the frothy aerated water. He kept his body and his reflexes loose, leaning into the current's turns as if he were riding a motorcycle through the rings of Saturn.

The Mirage sliced through to the flat, and Bolan was grinning like a triumphant teenage sports hero. He'd made it.

On a sudden whim he used a Duffek brace to head the Mirage back upstream. Named for the Czech kayaker who first demonstrated it thirty years earlier, it combined a leg-bracing maneuver with balance and hip movement to spin the boat around in a screaming turn, the paddle working for a moment as a fixed pivot.

A back eddy helped him upstream, but then Bolan cut back into the current, stroking furiously against the water's push. For a moment the Mirage hung almost motionless, then it slipped forward, and Bolan found himself surfing the last and highest of the row of standing waves.

He did not know how long he played in the white water, but finally, reluctantly, he moved on. There would be more waves—and bigger, and more challenging...much more challenging.

White-water rapids are classed by six degrees of difficulty, according to an accepted system that graded the river's steepness, roughness, volume, velocity and even its isolation. Class One rapids, the easiest, involved no major obstructions and only small riffles. Class Five rapids are labeled "extremely dangerous"; they involve huge standing waves, perilously positioned rocks and hydraulics strong enough to draw the biggest craft underwater.

Class Six rapids are impassable.

The Salmon was generally rated a Class Three river but, like any rating, this had to be taken as a rough guide only. Water level and volume varied, and so did the ratings. For now, the Corn Creek chart told the story: the river held lethal potential even for the

expert. Bolan would require all his resources of
strength and concentration. As a rule of thumb, he
could assume that every rapid was now a full class
above its midsummer rating.

Past Gunbarrel, Bolan drifted under the pack
bridge at Horse Creek, a suspension span about as
wide as a sidewalk; it was used by the professional
guides for their horses and mules. In water this high,
the deck of the bridge was no more than five feet
above Bolan's head. He could have reached up and
touched it with the blade of his long paddle as he
slipped beneath.

Beyond the bridge the river bent right and then
straightened, running due west for nearly two miles.
Near the end of this length Bolan could make out the
Tide Creek Lodge.

Here the canyon was a steep forested V, travers-
able only by river, or on foot or horseback over the
trail that was terraced into the mountainside above
the right-hand bank. The lodge itself, a majestic
three-story log structure with a wide veranda, stood
as a lasting memorial to someone's persistence and
elbow grease. A faint switchback road line above the
building was the clue: someone sometime had
brought heavy equipment overland to the ridge, then
crept it down along that crude road to a spot about
three hundred feet above the river. There, the
bulldozers and Cats had carved out a shelf on which
the buildings now sat. But the builders—the Kerrs,
Bolan wondered—had cared for the land on which
they had intruded. The site had been carefully reclaimed with native plants and framed by drainage

ditches, measures designed to keep erosion from getting a toehold.

A wooden stairway with handrails zigzagged down from the lodge. At its foot was a boathouse, a corrugated-tin shell on two pontoons topped with walkways, with a jet boat floating in the eddy between them. A short floating pier ran partway along the boathouse's riverside wall.

The lodge would be a damned nice spot for a man to get away to—and a fine place for a boy to grow. A boy like Johnny Kerr, Bolan remembered, thinking back on Miss Poten's fond look when she mentioned how he was temporarily in charge of the family operation. In this country a boy would learn to take on a man's work early in his days.

Then, as if an arctic chill had swept upriver, Bolan suddenly knew something was not right.

There were two guys in the shadow of the boathouse; one wore a pair of binoculars on a strap around his neck. Another half-dozen men were visible on the veranda of the lodge, apparently lounging around taking in the fresh air and scenery. At the distance of a half-mile they were not much more than shapes.

The guy with the binocs raised them in Bolan's direction and pointed, and his buddy put his mouth close to what looked like a Handie-Talkie. The men on the porch got up and filed into the house, and about then the steepness of the canyon cut off Bolan's view.

But he had already seen enough.

Whoever this group was, it was waiting for something.

Or someone.

Bolan's combat sense was flashing red alert.

He pulled up the right side of the spray skirt and dug out the little Detonics, resting the paddle across the deck as he slapped a .45 clip into the breech, the movement screened from the guys on the pier by his body in the resting, half-turned kayak now visible to them once more. The one with the binoculars still had him under surveillance. The dock was a quarter-mile distant, the swept kayak closing on it fast.

Bolan had covered another hundred yards when he heard the first shot.

6

The clean sharp crack of the rifle echoed off the canyon walls, but Bolan knew it had not been directed at him. He thought instantly of the Kerr youth, up there alone with a mob of men who were rapidly bearing out Miss Poten's assessment.

Then there were other things to worry about.

The second hardguy on the dock came out from behind the boathouse and leveled an autorifle in Bolan's direction.

A burst of slugs spit into the water five feet in front of the Mirage's bow.

Even if he had not been outclassed in firepower, Bolan saw no percentage in trying a shot from a moving boat at this distance. He yanked the zipper of the wet-suit jacket halfway down and stuck the Detonics inside, then braced hard left, wheeling his body and the kayak into the eddy and behind a car-sized boulder that gave him momentary cover.

It was a standoff but that wasn't good enough. The first rifle shot meant the boy up there was in danger for his life.

If he were not already dead.

Bolan had to believe he was alive—and in need of a friend double-quick.

He jerked the spray skirt all the way free, vaulted clear of the cockpit and dragged the boat up onto the craggy shore. Above him the canyon wall was a sheer rocky cliff, but it was the only way open to him. Screened from the gunmen's view, Bolan began to climb.

From the direction of the lodge he heard the shouts of men, and then a rapid-fire burst of gunfire.

Bolan had made five feet when something scraped rock above him. A pebble tumbled past his left ear. Bolan leaned out in time to see a length of rope drop down the cliff-face.

Then a figure came rappelling expertly down; the thick line passed under one thigh and across the body over the shoulder, legs kicking as he swung outward over the river, nearly in free-fall.

It was a youth in his teens. The Kerr boy.

And his rope ran out of length way above the rock-strewn shore.

But there was a ledge at that point, a foot wide at most, Bolan noticed. The boy reached it as quick as Bolan's thought process.

Autofire from the dock pulverized rock a few feet below the boy's position. All the gunner had to do was compensate for the radical muzzle-drop caused by the angle of fire, and he would pluck the sitting duck from his perch.

The boy never gave him the chance.

He bent his knees and pushed off in a soaring swallow dive over Bolan's head, his arms sweeping together as he plunged toward the rock-strewn river, slicing into it just upstream from Bolan's position.

The river closed over and ingested him.

Then the boy's head cut water directly in line with Bolan. The kid shook icy water from his face and swam hard for shore, making the eddy as Bolan clambered back down. The youth looked up at the tall figure in the black wet suit on the shore before him.

Bolan was already extending his paddle. "I'm a friend, Johnny."

The boy shivered once, then grabbed the proffered blade. "I gotta believe you." When he was close enough, Bolan reached out his right hand. The boy took it and scrambled out onto the rocks, crouching on hands and knees, his head down, trembling and breathing hard. "Thanks, mister." His voice quavered as the reality of what he had just done hit home. He shook violently, involuntarily.

Bolan knelt beside him...and caught a good look at his face for the first time.

Bolan gasped.

"Johnny?" he asked tentatively.

"How do you know my name, mister?"

"It can't be..." Bolan breathed.

The boy's expression narrowed with suspicion. "You all right?" he said.

Bolan stared, awestruck. He shook his head, trying to bring his mind back to the danger at hand. They were outnumbered, and the enemy had a vastly superior defensive stronghold, from above and ahead. The only logical response was retreat and, if possible, in a way that eliminated the threat of pursuit.

"I think they mean to kill you, mister," Johnny Kerr told him.

Bolan was still struggling to shake off the shock at what he had seen in Johnny Kerr's face, when a voice shattered the silence.

"Your attention!"

It was bullhorn amplified. It came from the lodge above them. The voice was without accent and strangely flat, without tonality.

"We know you are down there," the bullhorn announced. "If you turn yourself over to us this moment, we will not harm the young man. If you do not, you will both be killed."

"Don't trust 'em, mister. I saw what they—"

"This is your home turf, Johnny," Bolan interrupted. A lifetime of combat experience had reasserted himself. The mystery of this boy could wait. "How do we get out of here?"

"There's only one way—downriver."

"The jet boat. . . ."

"It won't run. They took out the rotor and distributor cap soon as I ferried them in yesterday. The spares, too."

And that made an already bad situation desperate. Unless Bolan disabled the boat so it was useless to the others, as well, they wouldn't get a mile downstream before they were caught and nailed.

"Is there a way to make it to the boathouse?"

"Follow me," Johnny Kerr said immediately.

"Hold on." The boy had to be kept out of it from here on as much as was possible. Whether Bolan wished it or not, the boy's life was suddenly in his hands.

"But I can show you—"

"I'll have to handle this one alone, Johnny," Bolan said, gently but firmly. "And I don't have time to argue."

The boy started to protest but caught himself. "See that big rock shaped like a tombstone? Just keep in line with it." Bolan started to move out, but the boy put a hand on his arm. "Just up from here I've got a kayak stashed in an old Indian rock shelter. Got me a wet suit and other gear, too. I guess I'd better get ready to use it."

"Good," said Bolan, pleased by the youth's preparedness. "But wait for me," he added, and dogtrotted off toward the boathouse.

He made the building's tin wall and plastered himself against it as he drew the Detonics. He took a breath, then spun around the end of the structure and onto the dock.

The guy with the binocs also had the radio now. He looked up from his conversation in time to see the Detonics spit flame. A .45 slug ripped through the little Handie-Talkie and cored on into the guy's brain, slamming him to the pier's deck in a gravy of body fluids peppered with microchips and shattered plastic. Beside him, the gunner spent a millisecond in fascinated examination of the mess, instead of concentrating on the business at hand, and that millisecond became an eternity when Bolan's second bullet caught him in the middle of the chest and spun him around to topple him from the dock. His soulless husk disappeared immediately in the current's whirling, frigid depths.

Somewhere above, multiple footsteps clattered on the wooden stairs.

Inside the boathouse's dimness, at the far end near the bobbing jet boat's stern, Bolan found two fifty-five-gallon drums of gasoline and a small hand pump. He unscrewed the bunghole caps on both and splashed fuel over the boat and the walkway. He used more to soak a rag, then ran a thick line near to the shed's door, where he was clear of the heavy fumes.

From the waterproof bag he took a cigarette and broke it in half before using the lighter on it. He carefully inserted the smoking butt in the rag, the lit end out.

The makeshift time fuse would give him maybe ninety seconds.

The men on the stairway were close enough now so that Bolan could make out individual voices.

Across the span of rocky shore he spotted a wet-suit-clad Johnny Kerr, standing with his own kayak where Bolan had left the Mirage.

"Get down, Johnny!" Bolan hollered.

The boy's figure disappeared behind the big boulder—and a heartbeat later autofire raked his position. Bolan scrambled in his direction, drawing fire himself, keeping as much cover as possible as he cut among the rocks.

When Bolan reached him, the boy was sitting on the coaming of his kayak, the boat bobbing in the shallows. He had set Bolan's Mirage next to him, ready for instantaneous launching. The boy was a cool thinker, for sure.

Bolan moved into his craft, snapping the spray skirt into place. "Be ready, Johnny," he clipped. Numbers counted off in descending order in his mind.

The men on the stairs reached the floating pier, and the thin air carried someone's shocked exclamation: "Jesus Christ, look what the guy did to Doc."

Bolan levered his paddle against a rock and said, "Let's go." The boy pushed off right behind him.

There were a half-dozen of them on the dock. Someone hollered and pointed in the direction of the two kayaks that had suddenly appeared, and the others had just enough time to turn and look.

What happened next made "what the guy did to Doc" seem like tender mercy in comparison.

The boathouse went up in a series of rippling explosions as, first, the rag ignited to send fire racing down the gasoline-impregnated walkway, and then the two storage barrels went, and lastly the tank of the jet boat itself. Corrugated metal tore with a banshee shriek, and jagged superheated pieces arced into the air and hissed into the river. The floating dock buckled under the impact of the concussion. Men tumbled into the life-numbing water. One or two might have been whole. The rest were maimed, their bodies rudely dissected and the wounds instantly and brutally cauterized by the red-hot, knife-edged tin that cut the air around them.

A thick curtain of steam rose from the river.

Bolan shot a look at Johnny Kerr. The boy's

mouth hung open, his eyes were wide with the awful reality of the scene. Bolan spoke his name.

Johnny spun around so quickly his kayak rocked violently, but instinctively he braced and kept from rolling. He blinked, and then he shut his mouth and muttered, "I'm all right, mister." Anticipating Bolan's order, he headed the bow of his boat and paddled toward the concealing steam, at the same time angling for the right bank away from the pulverized boathouse and the armed men in the lodge above it.

For a fraction of a moment Bolan stared after him, the image of the boy's face as he had first seen it burned into his mind's eye. It was impossible—and yet it was true.

Bolan stroked after him through the roiling river.

He had never met Johnny Kerr before; he was certain of that.

Yet the man knew the boy as he knew himself.

7

Mack Bolan looked into that face, and time peeled away like layers of paper unwrapped from a precious gift, and when he reached its core Bolan was back in time and space with another young man.

Back where it had all begun.

That other man was named Johnny as well— Johnny Bolan, kid brother to the man who would become known across his nation as The Executioner. In a way, Johnny was as responsible as any other person for launching the big brother he revered on his blitzkrieg assault on the Mafia.

Fate's implacable chain of events began one January, when Samuel Mack Bolan, steel-mill worker and loving father, suffered a mild heart attack that put him out of work for several weeks. The chain reaction reached critical mass the following August, when the Vietnam-based Sergeant Mack Bolan was called in by his company chaplain. The padre informed Bolan that he was being granted emergency personal leave.

His father, mother Elsa, and younger sister Cindy were dead. Brother John was in serious but stable condition in a Pittsfield hospital.

Forty-eight hours later Bolan stood beside the

youth's bed, grief for the dead and love for the living all mixed up with Johnny's obvious physical pain, which he was manfully struggling to overcome. When the nurse finally stopped bustling around and left them alone, Johnny told his big brother the stark facts.

Bolan listened grim faced to the tale of one good and loving and hard-working family's degradation and destruction at the hands of an inhuman criminal machine.

A man supported his people no matter how rough things were; that was how Sam Bolan saw it. Out of work and out of paychecks, he had borrowed money from some men with the Triangle Finance Company. These men were mafiosi; that was fact. Perhaps Sam Bolan knew, or at least suspected, but that did not matter. The payments that they demanded, grossly inflated by "vigorish," the usurious interest designed to make the borrower into a bond slave, were more than Sam Bolan could meet. Which was exactly what the Mafia shylocks expected and desired.

They did not want your money. They wanted your soul.

They got Sam Bolan's.

Somehow Cindy Bolan made contact with the men holding her father's I.O.U. She asked them to give him time, concerned that the stress would cause another, more massive, coronary attack. The men leered at the lovely pure seventeen-year-old girl-woman and offered her an alternative.

"She started working for those guys, Mack," Johnny said from his hospital bed. "She was...

sellin' herself. Don't look at me like that. I followed her one night and found out for myself.''

The discovery of his sister, huddled naked in a dingy hotel room with a flabby stranger three times her age, shattered Johnny. He did the only thing he could think of to stop her abasement, went to the only person in whose strength he could depend while his big brother was away at war.

He told his father.

Sam Bolan's first blind reaction was to punch his son in the mouth and call him a liar.

The commotion brought Cindy and Elsa into the living room. It did not matter Cindy told her father desperately, as Elsa tried to see to Johnny's bruised and bloodied mouth. After a few moments Sam Bolan suddenly fell silent, appeared to listen calmly to Cindy's story. He then left the room, returning a minute later.

In his fist was an old Smith & Wesson .45.

He shot Johnny first, but the boy remained conscious long enough to see him empty the rest of the weapon's load into Elsa and Cindy, the soft cherished bodies crumpling and quivering as the heavy slugs whumped into flesh. When the trigger fell on an empty chamber, Sam Bolan turned sad crazed eyes on his gravely wounded son.

"Sorry I busted your lip, John-O," he said calmly and went back to his bedroom.

Johnny lay there in his pain, the odor of cordite acrid in his nostrils. Time enough passed for his father to reload. Just before passing into blessed blackness, Johnny heard the last shot.

The one Sam Bolan used to take off the top of his own head.

During the next week, Mack Bolan, fresh from the jungle warfare of Southeast Asia, turned his deadly skills to bringing down the Pittsfield branch of the Cosa Nostra with cold military precision.

Dozens of the men who had visited Hell on the Bolan family, and so many good people like them, were dispatched to Hell themselves—and Johnny Bolan was given a new life. It came in the person of one Valentina Querente, 26, Pittsfield schoolteacher and angel of mercy, savior of Mack Bolan's life when she nursed him back to health after he was shot twice. Though she had given herself in love to no man before, she gave herself totally to this great gentle warrior. At the conclusion of the Pittsfield campaign, the love Bolan held for Johnny had expanded to encompass Val as well. She became the youth's legal guardian.

It was with great reluctance that Bolan left them, but there was no alternative. The life on which he determined to embark left no space for family, lover, or even friend. The Mafia's maggot presence in Pittsfield was duplicated across the country, and Bolan swore to do all that one man could to delouse his nation. He knew the Mob would never lie down for him to walk over; in a short time every resource of an inconceivably ruthless band of savages would be mobilized in an attempt to bring the Executioner to ground. Anyone close to him could be used as leverage.

Val took a teaching job at a private academy where

Johnny Bolan enrolled under an assumed name. No day passed that Mack Bolan did not think of his brother, but he was fated to look upon him and hold him close on only two more occasions since. Each was unexpected, and each was heart-wrenchingly bittersweet.

The last time was in St. Louis during the height of the Mafia war. The Executioner had come to the city on the Mississippi to carefully orchestrate, in his own best interests, the internecine scrap between the old-line forces of Arturo "Little Artie" Giamba and *La commissióne* representative Jerry Ciglia. Bolan was in the brutal center of the St. Louis showdown when he received a call from Leo Turrin. Leo was the *caporegime* of Pittsfield now—and also a highly placed federal undercover cop. He had been surreptitiously watchdogging Val and Johnny since Bolan's first strike had put the two men in contact.

Johnny Bolan was demanding a meeting with his big brother.

The circumstances and the timing were lousy, but Johnny would not be denied. The reunion took place in a St. Louis motel room, and there Johnny announced that he had determined to fight at his brother's side, and that he would not be turned away.

Bolan understood the youth's loneliness. The Mafia had robbed them of the rest of their family, but it was Bolan who was completing the job. He alone had made Johnny an orphan.

It was for the best, Bolan told him. Unless the boy were to live under a constant aura of danger, it would have to be this way. Johnny was frustrated, angered, saddened, but he would finally have to accept this glimmer of light instead of the total, life-snuffing darkness of constant fear.

When the balance had been restored in the Gateway City, Bolan turned back eastward in the big GMC RV he had converted into his War Wagon. He and Johnny spent a leisurely week returning to Pittsfield. Bolan let the youth take over much of the driving and cooking and housekeeping chores. They camped, fished and talked long into every night.

During that week Bolan's heart swelled with pride at the same time it ached with loss. This young man, blood of his blood, idolized him, looked up to him as only a brother can. On Bolan's part he saw before him an open, manly boy who would surely grow into a strong and true man, full of all the positive qualities of humanity for which Bolan fought.

Yet he would not be there to see the promise fulfilled.

In Pittsfield Mack Bolan turned Johnny over to Leo. He did not see Val, for there was only more pain in that direction. For long minutes the two brothers held each other wordlessly. Neither wanted to let go, yet both realized they must.

Bolan was giving a gift of freedom and a normal life to the youth. Johnny was giving his brother to the world.

And both knew that as soon as Bolan turned his back on Johnny, Bolan would stand face to face with Death. As a permanent condition in all of his remaining life, and miles.

Not long afterward, Johnny Bolan and Val Querente buried Mack Bolan.

Though there were no mortal remains, they held a simple ceremony on a windswept Wyoming butte, the two of them standing alone above the barren prairie. They did not dwell on what had been taken from them, but considered instead what Mack Bolan had given to so many before dying in the New York explosion.

In actuality Mack Bolan had denied Death its due. He fought on as John Phoenix.

Val Querente had married a G-man acquaintance of Leo Turrin. His name was Jack Gray, and right after the wedding he quit government service and opened a private law practice in Sheridan, Wyoming. Gray remained in touch with his old buddy, Leo, now safely removed from his double-agent life and riding a Department of Justice desk, so that through Leo, Bolan knew that Johnny was growing into the man he was destined to be. Nearly seventeen, he was filling out to the six-foot height and broad, hard physique of his brother. An outstanding scholar in high school, Johnny had also won letters in wrestling and track. In the summer the young man worked on the cattle ranch that his adoptive father maintained as a retreat outside Sheridan. According to Leo, he was becoming quite a cowboy, and this spring was expected to be an excellent calving season for the polled Herefords the father and son were raising.

Pride shone through Bolan's aching emptiness. Mack Bolan *was* dead—at least the Mack Bolan who could be brother to Johnny. But he lived on in the heart of the boy-turning-man who still mourned him.

That week-long trip from St. Louis to Pittsfield had been the last of anything like a vacation Bolan had allowed himself, until this Salmon River excursion now turned so deadly. If time were measured in battles fought and long war-miles walked, and in the deaths of so many of the evil for the salvation of the good—if time were counted as the sum of the bloody hours strung together along the Executioner's back-trail, then it had been aeons since Bolan had seen young Johnny.

But if time were measured by the intensity of feeling between two brothers, intensity that had never diminished, then scant moments separated the last of the Bolan men.

Now it seemed to Bolan as if they were close enough to touch once more.

THE RESEMBLANCE was uncanny.

Bolan stared at Johnny Kerr in the soft light of late afternoon. Full dark would not come for a while, but at the bottom of the steep Salmon River canyon, shadow began to spread early.

The youth was checking out his gear, sorting through it and putting aside whatever there was no immediate use for. His movements were sure-handed and businesslike as he absorbed himself in the task at hand, refusing to let his brush with death a few hours earlier compromise his effectiveness now.

He glanced up and smiled shyly at Bolan, and again the man saw the duplicate of that dear image he carried in his mind.

The image of Johnny Bolan.

Like that other faraway Johnny, the Kerr youth was partway through the perilous journey of the teen years, no longer a child, not yet a man. He was growing into that same broad, tall frame, and though still a little gawky with the last awkwardness of adolescence, he gave promise of developing into a man to be reckoned with. His dark hair was neatly trimmed, and the face below was open, honest and intelligent, quick to grin when a grin was called for. The high cheekbones, the determined set of his mouth, the intensity of his eyes—they were the cheeks and mouth and eyes of brother John.

"You're a pretty fair kayaker, mister," Johnny Kerr said.

"Not as good as you," Bolan said honestly.

"Good enough." Johnny's grin broadened. "Anyway, I've had plenty of time to practice."

By the waterproof chronometer on Bolan's left wrist, they had been on the river about three hours; the river log and map he carried showed they had covered about twenty miles. There had been no sign of pursuit yet, but Bolan had wanted to put plenty of space between them and the Tide Creek Lodge, for the sake of Johnny Kerr's safety.

Yet he knew this fight was far from over.

The pristine wilderness of the River of No Return was now The Executioner's latest hellground.

With the adrenaline still pumping through their veins, Bolan and Johnny had hit Ranier Rapids a few miles below the lodge. Ranier was at least a class bigger than Gunbarrel, and Bolan let the river-savvy youth go first, following him through the right-hand channel. The goal now was speed not thrills, so Johnny guided him to the left of the line of four-foot-high standing waves that attempted to grab at them and impede their progress. He found the channel, paddling as effortlessly as if this were a pond instead of a raging torrent of swirling, sucking white water. Near the end of the run Johnny used a Duffek pivot to broach his boat, then deliberately braced upstream so that the current rolled him over, under, then up again. Just for the hell of it. Perhaps he was testing himself, or even showing off a little for Bolan's benefit, but it was a good sign. Whatever kept the boy's confidence up was all to the good.

Then, as Johnny came out of the rapids, Bolan saw the boy back-paddle hard to bring the forward motion of his boat to a stop. Bolan pulled up beside him.

Hooked on a sharp branch of a log snag piled against the left bank was a waterlogged bundle of red-stained clothing. It was the remains of what had once been the body of the hardboy gunner on the pier. If the bullet wound had not been fatal, the water had. Unprotected human flesh would begin to frigidify within minutes in the snowmelt of the river.

"Let's go," Bolan said gruffly, paddling past the boy. Johnny was quick behind him.

They glided past the Lantz Bar Guard Station, unmanned until early summer. Beyond, they expertly negotiated Big and Little Devil's Teeth, where the jagged rocks from which the rapids took their names peeked just above the surface at this time of year.

The lower of the two rapids shot them out just below the Guth's outfitting cabin, from which squads of hunters and fishermen took off in season.

Somewhere ahead, the constant rush of the river became a rising roar, and from Bolan's vantage point the water seemed to abruptly disappear.

Johnny pulled into the eddy. "Salmon Falls," he announced. He had to raise his voice to be heard over the noise. "If we've got time we ought to take a break before we run it." He grinned. "It's a man-eater."

Bolan circled thumb and forefinger, held the other three fingers stiff in an "okay" sign. The river bent right, and past a little creek coming in on the other side there was another small bench called Corey Bar, site of a Forest Service campground. Bolan could see a few tables and an outhouse set back in the juniper at the foot of the steep slope. They eased their kayaks on to the access at the campground's lower end, caught the eddy and docked among the rocks.

Bolan climbed stiffly out of the cockpit, stretching legs that had gone half numb from the tension of bracing and the monotony of the cramped position within the bowels of the boat. His arms were feeling it; simply holding up a double-bladed kayak paddle for three consecutive hours taxed the muscles. The cold and the wetness was another factor, despite the neoprene Wilderness Seasuit, which was the best available; it worked by trapping a layer of water next to the skin, where it was warmed by body heat to serve as a layer of insulation. Over the long run the neoprene was effective protection against exposure and hypothermia, and had been used to good effect by Bolan's Phoenix Force in their mission beneath the Atlantic waves. But each time a wave crashed over Bolan or he did an Eskimo roll, a fresh wash of frigid water replaced the warmed-up supply inside the suit, and the shock of it was enough to take his breath away.

Yet there was something correct and purposeful in these minor pangs and discomforts. Despite the man-madness upriver, despite the responsibility for the boy, which had been thrust upon him, Bolan felt invigorated, warm with a glow of intense energy that encompassed him with far greater actuality than the venal murderousness of the lodge fight.

Now Johnny Kerr, squatting across the little camp clearing, dug into his Bills Bag. "Can we have fire?" he asked Bolan. He pulled out a Coleman backpack stove.

Daylight would be fighting the deepening shadows a while longer, and they were shielded from the river here. Beyond that, Bolan was hungry for something more than the sweet taste of the appetite-whetting mountain air.

"Some hot food would go good," Johnny said.

For sure. It would keep their strength up as well.

They would need it.

8

For millenia people have come into the wilderness canyon of the River of No Return seeking the soothing balm of meditation, striving to meld the purity of the land with that of an open mind. Perhaps first were the ancient cave-dwellers, five thousand years before Christ; later, for sure, came the manly, peace-loving Nez Percé. Then, even among the Europeans, were some men who brought a humble respect to this land. Such men tried to live in harmony, not to despoil. Race did not matter; and if those who came were true and large and dedicated to a life of confirmation, the river sometimes bestowed on them the gift of vision.

Now Mack Bolan closed his eyes for a moment and became one with the land and its spirit. He did not sleep, nor did he dream, but images took over and occupied his mind, and Bolan heard the Voice of the River and listened.

It is daylight, and the river is an eternal flowing highway of roiling water without beginning or end. Its constant roar is full of heady pride; it is a cockcrow, or the bugle of a bull elk. Mack Bolan paddles. His muscles bulge with an effusion of strength; his face is set in a rictus of determination. He does not know how long he has been paddling under the thin spring-time sun: hours, maybe days—perhaps all his adult life. Mack Bolan knows only that were he able to reach the terminus of this dangerous voyage, it would make no difference; there will always be other rivers, other dangers.

But this time it is different, and suddenly he remembers why. Bolan twists around in the kayak's tight cockpit. Yes, there is the boy, paddling his own canoe not far off Bolan's stern. They began this trip with urgency, Bolan recalls; The Executioner still wears the checkered wool shirt in which he arrived on Salmon River, with machine pistol holstered under his left arm. The boy has a pack on his back and strapped to it is a long, handsome game rifle with a scope, black and long as a cudgel. The boy lives in this country and is at ease in it.

The boy looks up and flashes Bolan a grin that is shy and confident all at the same time. The grin says, "We will reach the end of this violent river after all, my big friend. Just as you have reached the end of so many other violent roads in your day. Do not worry, big brother."

Brother. Mack Bolan is momentarily disconcerted. Once he had a brother, but that was before. This other boy is named Johnny, like his brother, and reminds Bolan of him. Indeed, the two could be twins. Bolan's mind churns as fast as his paddle. Is the spirit of the river playing a trick on him? Is the boy behind him a stranger, or his true flesh-and-blood kin?

There comes a warm suffusing glow that spreads throughout his body, and the truth and the worth of kinship and humanity now course through Bolan's veins.

Then he hears the first burst of gunfire.

Bolan turns in his seat again, so hard that the kayak almost dumps, and only a quick instinctive hip-snap keeps him upright. Fifty yards upriver, in the channel and on their backtrack, is an inflated rubber raft. Four life-jacketed men ride its bobbing, bucking form. Each holds a black ugly-snouted submachine gun. In the millisecond it takes Bolan to absorb all this, one man unlooses another quick slash of deadly lead in their direction.

The boy, the vision whispers urgently. *The boy is everything. If the boy is killed, it is your ultimate defeat, Mack Bolan. You will be a walking dead man, condemned to live out all the rest of your days in grief and fear and collapse, and the world around you will rot like so much decomposing offal, because you failed to protect this one precious life.*

"Get your head down, Johnny!" Bolan hollers. "Paddle for your life. All we need is a few seconds—they can't catch us in the raft."

But Johnny ignores him. He digs in his pack and comes out with a revolver, and dropping his paddle he returns fire. He aims carefully, taking his time before squeezing off each shot. Yet

Bolan knows with infinite despair that the odds
are insurmountable: a boy against four men, a
short-barreled handgun against chattering auto-
rifles.

Everything slows, as if for Bolan's benefit, as
if someone wishes him to see every horrendous
detail of what happens next. The rubber raft
bobs over a low rock and into a smooth eddy, no
waves to upset the men's aim. The four raise
their automatic weapons together and wait a
single beat. Then they fire simultaneously,
holding down triggers to empty magazines completely, and a virtual cloud of lead descends
upon and envelops the boy Johnny.

A ragged animal scream rips from Mack
Bolan's throat, a sound bereft of humanity and
full of anguish and dread and despair.

Mack Bolan opened his eyes with a start. He could
hear his scream echoing off the canyon walls, although he knew this was only an aftereffect of his vision. On the plane of reality he had made no actual
sound.

Johnny Kerr sat opposite with his legs folded
under him. He was heaping beef stew and green
beans in butter sauce onto an aluminum plate. He offered it, giving Bolan a curious look. Bolan blinked
and shook the strange daylight nightmare out of his
mind.

"I guess I dozed off for a few seconds," Bolan
said, taking the plate.

Johnny shrugged. "Could be." He seemed to be

considering what he was about to say. "Sometimes when I'm in this country I get the feeling that the river is almost...well, almost alive...like it had a soul or something." He looked up at Bolan again. "Sometimes I even think it's talking to me, in a way. Guess that's kind of dumb, huh?"

"The Indians didn't think it was dumb, Johnny."

Johnny nodded. "I had a hunch you'd understand."

Yeah, Bolan understood. The river spirit had not presented him with some unalterable vision of the future; it was simply alerting him to the danger ahead. Johnny Kerr's life was in his hands; for Bolan, that life must be more valuable than his own. He could not—*would not*—see this boy killed before his eyes.

He would teach the youth what he needed to know. He would teach him instinctively, by his very presence. And if that male magic failed to work, Bolan would meet an enemy victory by giving up his own life first.

That was Mack Bolan's answer to the river's vision-message; that was his pact with the river's spirit.

Inscribed and sealed, and signed in blood.

Johnny had whipped up the meal on a little Coleman white-gas stove, no more than six inches high and five wide, but capable of boiling a quart of water in four minutes. The food had come from Mountain House foil pouches, freeze-dried to a quarter of its original weight and given a virtually infinite shelf life. To Bolan, at this moment, it tasted as good as homemade. He ate it in silence.

Johnny put more water on for coffee. Bolan settled back with his plate against a ponderosa-pine log.

"Johnny," he said evenly, "I must know everything that you know about what happened at the lodge."

The youth forked a last piece of beef into his mouth and chewed on it thoughtfully. It was the same cautious quality Bolan had seen in Miss Poten, the Western habit of measuring one's words, to ensure the proper slowness in making a judgment or taking offense and then of speaking plainly what had to be said.

"I took a disliking to them right off," Johnny admitted. "As soon as I pulled the jet boat up to the Corn Creek dock I had second thoughts. I guess it was their gear, first off. Most people come in with packs—some of the dudes even bring suitcases—but they had these wooden crates, enough of them so it took three trips to get them up to the lodge. And they were making it clear they didn't want me snooping around or asking questions—not that I would have anyway.

"Second, was the way they acted. There were a lot of them, more than thirty, and every one of them was an obvious novice. I offered to take them uptrail, maybe find a high-country stream flowing gentle enough so they could snap a few trout, but they weren't interested. They weren't interested in anything except sitting around and keeping to themselves. But they were the paying guests, a windfall at this time of year for the cash register, and I'd promised mom and pa I'd see to whatever they wanted, so that was that.''

Johnny paused at the thought of his parents, then continued with a stronger voice.

"Naturally I had to be around in case they wanted something, but they didn't pay me much mind, I guess because they thought I was just a kid. So I heard them talking, and I found out they were waiting for someone. I didn't know what exactly for, but I got the feeling it wasn't to give him a brass-band welcome. That was you, wasn't it?''

Yeah, it looked like it was. Bolan nodded.

"Then I saw what was inside one of the crates," continued Johnny. "It was filled with M-16 rifles."

"Are you sure that's what they were?" Bolan asked.

"Mister, on Salmon River guns are tools, and if you want to make it you better know something about them—all kinds of them.''

There was no boast in the youth's tone, only a simple statement of fact.

"I ordered them off the property," Johnny said stoutly. "Those guns, along with what I had heard and what my hunch told me, added up to something that smelled worse than gut-shot deer meat. We weren't so broke that we had to take their kind of money.''

"What happened?"

"They laughed at me," Johnny said angrily. "They laughed, so I fetched my pa's 30.06 hunting rifle, and they stopped laughing. But one of them got behind me and tried to take it away. I fired, but I didn't hit any of them.''

"Did it occur to you," Bolan asked as neutrally as he could, "that at thirty-or-so to one, they had you a little outnumbered?"

"The lodge is my place," Johnny said immediately, "mine and my people's. It's where I live, and those men had come to it just to start trouble. The only thing I knew was that something had to be done."

"I understand, Johnny. What happened then?"

"I had to get free, go for help. That's when you came along. I managed to tear loose and outrun them. None of them is in real good shape, and anyway the altitude can get to you if you're not used to it. You know the rest."

Johnny found collapsible aluminum cups among his supplies and spooned in instant coffee, then added boiling water and handed one to Bolan.

"You must have been expecting some kind of trouble," Bolan suggested. He gestured at the gear spread out between them. Besides the stove, plates, utensils and rations, there was a sleeping bag, a compact one-man tube tent, first-aid gear and water purification tablets, a couple of changes of woolen clothing, hiking boots, a knife, and a small tool kit, all carefully arranged in waterproof bags. Johnny's kayak, stashed in the rock shelter, had been rigged out so he could take off instantly and be fully equipped for a voyage of several days at any time of the year.

Again Johnny considered his answer. "Not trouble exactly," he said slowly. "I always feel better when

I'm ready. For anything. See, here in the back country you have to pay a little more mind when it comes to surviving. I've always kept this kayak ready, since I was big enough to sit in the cockpit without being swallowed up. Sure, we've got the jet boat. But it needs gas to run, and it's too easy to knock out—just like happened today. But a kayak...well, as long as you're more or less in one piece, a kayak will get you downriver. As long as you know how to use it." He smiled.

Bolan gazed at the young man with respect. The resemblance to his brother was more than physical. It was of the mind, too, and of the spirit, growing.

The youth continued. "But sometimes being ready, and surviving, isn't enough." There was steel in his voice. "Those men ran me off my own place. I've got to do something about that."

Agreed, Bolan thought to himself. Sometimes survival was not enough. A man could dig a hole in the ground and climb in and cover it over, and that was survival—but for what? Long ago Mack Bolan had decided that survival was pointless without change— without growth. That was why he had risked his personal survival so many countless times: because sometimes a man had to be willing to die for the survival of the world.

Or willing to kill. To kill for the elimination of destruction.

Yeah, indeed, Mack Bolan knew how Johnny Kerr felt.

Staring at the boy through the deepening evening shadows, Bolan felt the eerie sense of kinship grow stronger. Johnny Kerr's calmness and his determination seemed so much like himself, even, that the nightfighter might have been looking through the semiopaque window of his own years.

Despite his decision to put the safety of the boy first, they might have no choice but to stay and fight. In the course of events, the battle-seasoned warrior and the courageous young woodsman might be forced into battle to avenge the wrong visited upon Johnny Kerr. And to face together a full-assault hit-team assassination attempt upon Mack Bolan.

"How did you know my name, mister?" Johnny broke into his thoughts.

Bolan almost told him all of it, including his resemblance to the other Johnny, and what that meant. Instead he mentioned his hamburger lunch at Miss Poten's.

"Well," Johnny said, "I can't go on calling you 'mister' like you're one of my parents' guests."

Automatically Bolan began to say, "John Phoenix." He stopped himself. In a real way this young man was already a comrade-in-arms, and for that reason alone he would extend a small but heavy piece of honesty to him.

"The name is Mack. Just Mack."

Johnny offered his hand, and Bolan took it. The young hand was already slightly calloused with hard work, the grip firm.

"What's the plan, Mack?"

"To get downriver for help."

"But what they *did* . . . we've got to—"

"They've got firepower, manpower and position

on us." Bolan lit a cigarette in the flame of the Coleman stove. "There are some fights you can't win, at least not by charging into them feet first and eyes closed. That's a hard fact to swallow at first, young John, but after a while you get it down. This is one of those fights."

But Johnny Kerr was no longer paying attention. He was sitting up from the log, his eyes narrowed, his head perfectly still.

"Hear it?" he whispered.

Yes, Bolan heard it, almost imperceptible at first, the noise coming toward them from upriver. It was the low grumble of an engine, maybe engines, the cacophonous mechanical sound alien among the natural sounds of water and wind and evening insects that had, until then, been alone with them in the canyon. The on-land engine noise was still some distance away, but its volume was steadily increasing.

Bolan glanced at Johnny. The boy seemed a little frightened, but a lot ready.

It was a good mental state to carry into war. And war it would soon be.

The decision was out of their hands.

Bolan tamped out his cigarette in the sand and stood up. In a sense he was relieved. He was not accustomed to retreat and evasion. He had learned long ago that no matter how fast or how far you run from an enemy, you never get anywhere until you stand your ground and fight.

The running here was over. The war was engaged. It was time to wrench the gun barrels around and let the aggressors take a long slow look into their black depths.

The Executioner was stalking Salmon River country. And on this night, for some men, the River of No Return would live up to its name.

9

Motorized travel was strictly prohibited on this trail of the Nez Percé National Forest.

Right now, the penalty for violation of that rule was execution.

If the third rider in the file of motorcycles had done much biking before, it was on city pavement. The trail carved into the side of the slope was washboard dirt studded with half-exposed rocks and crossed with tree roots like speed bumps. Instead of finding a rhythm to ride out the roughness, the guy was fighting the trail every foot of the way, twisting furiously at the handlebars, alternately gunning the engine and tromping on the brakes, spewing dirt and acrid exhaust fumes and angry obscenities into the sweet spring air.

He had just crested a little rise and was perhaps a hundred feet above the river, when Mack Bolan stepped out from behind a twisted juniper, directly in front of him.

The biker had time to look up and that gave Bolan his target. He was carrying a five-foot deadfall branch of heavy larch.

Bolan swung the branch into the guy's Adam's apple like a home-run hitter going for the upper decks.

The wood cracked sharply and one end flew off into the shadows as the guy flopped over on his back. The bike sputtered on and out from under him before toppling angrily to the ground.

The biker opened his mouth and made raspy sounds. His voice box and windpipe were both crushed. Bolan could read the man's foreknowledge of his fate in his horrified eyes: two or three minutes of impotent airless agony before the mercy of suffocation.

Bolan rolled the guy over on one side, knelt behind him as he drew the Buck knife on his left hip. Case-hardened steel carved a gash through skin and neck muscle and jugular vein, and the all-forgiving blessedness of death banished pain forever.

Bolan wiped the knife clean on the guy's woolen shirt. On the gunner's hip in custom leather was an Ingram M-11 machine pistol, the square-cut full-automatic smaller than a service .45. Bolan dropped out the clip and saw that it was fully loaded with steel-jacketed .380 shorties. He reseated the magazine and tucked the little room-broom inside his wet-suit jacket.

The shadows were lengthening more rapidly now; full dark was minutes away. But the sky had been cloudless all day and the moon had already climbed into the eastern sky. It would be a clear bright night.

The guy's bike was a Honda Trail 90 that looked brand-new, the excess injection-molded rubber on the deep-tread all-terrain tires still sticking out from the sidewalls like chin whiskers. Bolan righted the machine, kicked it back to life and mounted up.

The trail had left the riverside several miles back to climb to this ridge. Just below Bolan's present position was a series of switchbacks ending on a bench, and below that a little sandy bar on the right bank, the site of the Guth outfitting cabin that he and Johnny had passed earlier before putting in. Bolan stopped the bike on the ledgelike bench, set it on its kickstand but left the little engine puttering.

He descended silently.

The two other bikers were in front of the cabin, trying to make out a map in the moonlight. Bolan could hear their voices. "Looks like the trail cuts north away from the river starting here," one of them said. He wore a rolled-brim black wool cap and a matching turtleneck.

"So?" his partner asked. Both wore side arms in belt holsters.

"So this is the end of the line for us."

In more ways than one, Bolan thought.

"That's okay with me. I'm ready to head back. These woods give me the creeps."

"Weren't you ever a Boy Scout?"

"Nah. I scouted for girls."

The other man did not laugh. He was staring up thoughtfully at the unchanging sound of the motorbike. "Webster?" he called.

"He's probably taking a leak."

"Webster!" More sharply.

Night insects and the echo of his own voice were the only replies.

"Take cover," the guy muttered.

So they had discipline. The guy in the hat was the

apparent leader of this recon; he leaped the few steps
to the far edge of the sandbar and dropped behind
the protection of a log. Bolan saw the flash of gun-
metal. The other guy slid noiselessly into the shadow
of the outfitting cabin.

Bolan began working around the bar from his
position above it.

"Webster," the guy behind the cabin called.

"Shut up, Kirkness," the leader ordered.

"Let's just get the hell out of here."

"When I say so."

Bolan was about fifteen feet above the leader when
the ledge ran out. The slope was crumbly gravel,
steeper than a house roof.

"It's him, ain't it," Kirkness whispered from the
shadow of the cabin, his voice dire with distraught
nerves.

"Shut up," the leader said again.

Bolan was fully exposed—if anyone was sharp-
eyed enough to pick out his immobile black figure
from the darkness of the moss-covered rocks and the
trees around him. The idea was to avoid gunfire if at
all possible. He had no way of knowing how close the
others in this venomous group might be, and along a
canyon the report of gunfire could carry for miles.

"I say we move on out," Kirkness insisted.

"You listen to me," the leader began, his voice rising in anger—and his concentration that much
diluted.

Bolan launched himself out from the ledge, hit the
slippery gravel ten feet below to ski the last of it
on the rugged soles of the Tabata Wet Shoes. The

bike-squad leader started to spin to face him, but Bolan came upon him like a sliding base runner. He slammed his forearm against the guy's right wrist, and his weapon skittered away across hardpan dirt. The guy tried to bring his knee up, but Bolan's arm moved in again too quickly, digging for the guy's side.

The knife blade went in just below the bottom rib. Bolan twisted it hard and felt the guy's last hot breath in his face. He got the guy by the arm and spun him around before he could go down, withdrawing the knife against the suction pull of flesh and organ as he did so, propping the guy's dead-weight up against himself.

Ten feet across the sand, Kirkness spun around in time to see Bolan level the little Ingram on him from behind the protection of his boss's figure. The guy began to bring his own gun up, hesitated, and then swore out loud in panic and despair, knowing that the hesitation had cost him the play—and probably his life.

"Drop it," Bolan ordered. His voice was as chilling as the river water. "Drop it or your buddy gets it." Bolan held one hand clamped over the corpse's wound to cut off the blood flow. It was a bluff, but in the dusk it had a fair chance of working.

If it didn't, he would blow the guy away and take the chance of the consequences.

But it did.

"Lenny. . . ." the guy appealed for advice.

"Drop it."

The guy's gun thudded into the sand.

Bolan let Lenny's limp body slump.

"Well, shit," Kirkness said in disgust.

Bolan stepped over the log barrier, his face granite hard. He gestured with the barrel of the Ingram.

Kirkness looked at the river and turned paler.

"Move," the chill-sender ordered.

Kirkness stepped back toward the water. Bolan crowded him; Kirkness took more steps back. River water lapped at the ankles of his hiking boots.

Bolan flicked the Ingram's stubby barrel impatiently.

Kirkness took another step and the water boiled around his calves. Bolan shook his head. The next step took the guy into a little hole, and the water went above his knees.

The guy's face was as gray as the ashes of a campfire.

"I can't swim!" he blurted.

"You won't have to," Bolan told the guy. "The cold will get you first."

"Jesus God. Just shoot me and get it over with."

Bolan waved the gun.

The terrified guy hesitated, then took another backward step. Water lapped at his crotch.

"I can't feel my toes. Oh, God," the guy wailed.

"Who's in charge, Kirkness?" Bolan cut in.

Faint hope cut terror in the guy's eyes. "Lenny? He's just the...."

"Talking and breathing. You stop doing one, and I'll stop the other. Get it? Who's in charge? Tell me now."

"He calls himself Vigoury. He acts like a guy

who's been around and knows what he's doing. That's all I got on him, God's truth."

"Describe him."

"Tall, maybe your height. Dark wavy hair, darkish complexion. Talks without an accent, but sometimes the way he puts words together doesn't sound quite right.

"How do you fit into this?"

"After Nam I got out and started working on my own, pickup jobs here and there, for the money. You know how it is."

Yeah, Bolan knew. "You're a disgrace to the uniform, guy," he said. "How were you contacted?"

"Through people I knew, a series of mail drops—the usual. Listen, man, my feet are starting to freeze solid, I swear to God."

"In a few minutes they will freeze. If you live, you'll wheel yourself around on a board the rest of your life, staring at the stumps and wishing you'd talked faster."

"I'm telling you what you want. Lemme out of here!"

"Who are the others?"

"I only knew two of them, one guy named Gornick, 'nother named Salvatore. The first contact was a couple months ago. After that we only got together once. It was weird. We met in Rome, and then they flew us all to some camp in the desert—never told us where. This Vigoury checked us out, ran us through some drills, no big deal. Except he seemed like he was being awful damned careful—and he had plenty of money to spend. We got back to the States and we were supposed to be on call. So day before yesterday the call comes, we meet in Salt Lake, a private plane flies us into Salmon, we get in this school bus and here we are.''

''Why?''

''We're supposed to kill a guy. One guy and thirty of us. In front of Vigoury everyone's real serious, but when he's out of earshot no one figures you need an army to take out one guy. Maybe we was wrong.''

The venal ex-soldier tried to laugh at his own joke, and instead his teeth began to chatter, his jaw out of control.

''Why?''

''Why what?''

''Why kill me?''

''Oh, God. For money—look, I'm being straight, like you said. I'm cold. They didn't tell us anything about why, we didn't ask. Vigoury said there wouldn't be any kickback, and I didn't think about it past that.''

''Maybe you should have.''

''Guess so,'' the guy agreed.

''Where is he?''

Kirkness's teeth clacked like a Spanish dancer's castanets. ''Vigoury's with the others, I guess. Left them at the lodge.'' The guy was getting light-headed from the cold. His words starting to slur. In a moment he would start babbling, anything to get out of the water. Bolan had to find out the rest in a heartbeat.

''More,'' he rapped.

''Vigoury was s'posed to radio, get 'nother jet boat

from somewhere, North Fork, the outfitter. Coming after you and the kid, sooner or later. What'd you ask me? Can't...."

"Come out of there," Bolan ordered.

The guy lurched a half-step toward the shore, stiff as the Frankenstein monster in an old movie. "Can't...legs...don't wanna work right...."

Bolan shoved the Ingram inside the wet suit. The guy was already incapacitated, alertness draining from him as his circulation faltered.

He waded into the water, extending his hand.

But instead of waiting for him, the guy lurched at that hand, staggered, lost his footing, pitched forward into the iciness.

His fingertips grazed Bolan's.

The current immediately caught him and swirled him away from Bolan. Then the force of the main channel took its turn. The scared gunner's arms and legs flailed leadenly against the power of the dark, swollen, churning river.

The guy managed to find breath for a hellish scream that resounded between the canyon walls. In the moonlight Bolan could see him being swept over a rock eddy and into the suckhole on its other side.

He would not emerge. The terrible waters would jealously retain their prey deep within their grinding hydraulics, with a power as unfathomable and eternal as the mountains that towered around them.

Bolan stared at the boiling, moonlit river. He remembered the words uttered by Miss Jane Poten that very day. *The wild country's got ways of gettin' back at folks like that. Sometimes they're mean, and not always pretty.*

Bolan began to pick his way back, rock by rock along the shore, downstream to the Corey Bar camp where he'd left Johnny Kerr.

Vigoury.

The name rang some faint alarm deep in the back of Bolan's mind.

Vigoury.

Briefly scanned files, seemingly incidental cross-references, came to focus.

Vigoury.

Bolan knew where he had seen that name before. And he knew what it meant.

More blood, much more blood, would certainly flow down Salmon River before this night was through.

10

"Vigoury!"

Aaron Kurtzman spun around in his swivel chair, and the triumphant smile on his face dimmed only slightly when he realized he was alone in the War Room. He turned back to his terminal, scanned the data displayed across the green-tinted video tube, typed in a final instruction. In a corner of the room the "daisy wheel" font of a line printer began to race back and forth as sprocket-hole-edged copy rolled out of the top of the machine.

Kurtzman picked up a phone, push-buttoned a number, paused, said, "April, can you come down here for a minute? . . . Yes, I think so."

The Bear had barely enough time to load his pipe, search out matches in one of his voluminous pockets and get the tobacco glowing before April stepped through the inside portal of the double-interlocking doors. Harold Brognola was close on her heels. He had been on-site since that morning, acting as liaison with the NSC team investigating the Nevada hit.

"What have to got, Aaron?" April took a seat at the conference table, Brognola lowering his bulk into the chair opposite.

"I'm not sure," Kurtzman confessed, "and I

don't want you to get too excited. I do have some data on those two men who tried to jump Mack on U.S. 93, and it projects some answers to our other questions. But—and this is a big but—there is a statistical probability of about seventy-five percent that the projection is entirely correct. In computational terms, as you know, April, that's little more than an electronic hunch.''

"It's a start," April said.

"It is that," Kurtzman agreed. "Something we know for sure is the identity of one of the ambushers. We got as far as Interpol in Europe before it turned up. He was a West German national named Konrad Richter, age 27, military service, honorable discharge. He ran a martial arts academy in Bonn, and also tutored private students in hand- and long-gun techniques. All legal, no police record. However, he was suspected of having been in the company of known members of the Baader-Meinhof terrorist gang.''

"The other guy probably had a similar background," Brognola suggested. "Clean record, even if he did have some fishy associations. Military veteran, knowledge of weapons and experience in using them—and willing to do so, on anyone, for a price.''

"That's the line of speculation I followed," Kurtzman said. "And it brought me to one Vigoury.''

"What sort of a name is that?''

"It's the only name we've got.'' Kurtzman relit his pipe, tossed the match at an ashtray and missed. "When Mack took out Frank Edwards in that Tripoli villa, you'll remember he started out going in soft. He managed to obtain a computer printout of all of Edwards's personnel files—other renegade agents, terrorist connections he'd made, even a list of prospective operatives for the 'black CIA' that Edwards was trying to set up. One of the names on that list was Vigoury.

"Even with the help of the boys over at the NSC," Aaron continued, "it's taking me time to get such a wealth of material analyzed. Mack saw the raw data, however, and he recognized a few names that helped push us in some of the right directions. Still, we're not finished sifting through it yet."

"But so far," April pressed, "what do we have on Vigoury?"

"Enough to realize we aren't dealing with your common garden-variety gunpunk—and enough to know we aren't going to find much more. Vigoury is a shadow man: nationality, past history, political affiliation, all unknown. Even less of a record than Richter, the dead German. It's as if he didn't exist until very recently. Although the connection would be too well camouflaged to uncover easily, I'd guess he was originally in the control of the USSR, a created killer. That is, a man raised and trained all his life for one purpose and kept under wraps until that purpose presented itself."

"The Russians loaned him out to the terrorist network?" April asked.

"Undoubtedly," Brognola put in, rhyming with Kurtzman's nod. "That would be the 'purpose presented.' The terrorists get all the good stuff nowadays."

"And his first assignment. . ." April breathed.

". . . is to kill John Phoenix," Kurtzman finished for her.

The line printer fell silent. Aaron moved to it, ripped off a length of accordion-folded copy and set the paper in front of April.

"You can look that over at your convenience," he said, "but the gist of what the computer is saying is this: the two in Nevada were clean as the guns they were carrying, and mostly untraceable—like Vigoury. They comprised an advance team, and if they failed—as they did—there would be backup troops for a second attempt, and perhaps others after that. With nothing showing up for law enforcement. Vigoury's been recruiting, we know that much. But cleanly again—triple-removed initial contact, double call-back, so the applicants don't get near him until he's had them checked out to the labels on their jockey shorts.

"One thing that bothers me, though," Kurtzman added. "Why didn't his Russian masters just give him a squad of their own men?"

"Two reasons," April offered immediately. "One, a whole gang of Reds forming an international assassination team is too risky politically. They couldn't do it any more than we could. The potential uproar is too dangerous. Two, men like Vigoury take years, not to mention millions of rubles, to create. They come in limited editions, not in mass productions."

"That's for sure," Hal said. "Aaron, what do we know about the other applicants?"

"They were all of the same general stripe. Ex-servicemen with a beef, or heavy bills, or just bored with the civilian rat race. Agents, either active, retired, or renegade. Callous mercenaries. Active terrorists with no record as yet. Shadow people, like Vigoury. Sad to say, every damned one of them should have a record but none of them does.''

"Okay," April said, looking at each of them in turn. "Here's the sixty-four-thousand-dollar question: how did those two in Nevada get on to Mack's trail? How did they know he was coming through there?''

Brognola rubbed wearily at the bridge of his nose with thumb and forefinger. "Someone spotted him in Dulles, or at the Salt Lake City airport.''

"Spotted him? What do you mean, 'spotted him'?'' April's brows furrowed.

"We think the terrorist net has a make on Striker," Brognola revealed. He met April's hard gaze. "I don't think they know his name or sanction, and I know for certain the base here is secure. But there are enough eyewitness and survivor reports of Mack's recent hits now for some cross-referencing to be going on. They know it's the same man—they may even have a composite sketch of him. It's possible, although not probable, that he's been photographed. They've got a file on him, a pattern profile. Knowing what they do, they are willing to spend a lot of time and money to have him killed.''

April's face trembled in sadness, her hair falling about her bowed head to conceal her eyes. Then she raised her face in anger, eyes blazing. "Why wasn't I informed of this development?" Passion glowed in her features. "As operations director of Stony Man Farm—" she glared at Hal "—I should have been briefed on this as your Intelligence developed."

"You're being briefed now," Brognola said, but his manner was deferential; he raised his hands in supplication and apology. "The incident in Nevada, along with the connections it developed to Vigoury, has moved the possibility of Mack's top billing on a hit-list out of the realm of idle speculation, and into the sphere of probability. That is what I am saying. But he's been there before: in fact he's there all the time—the sphere of probable death. Statistically, which is to say by the law of averages, we've known that all along. Of course, Mack has not been an average fighter."

"The basis of the Stony Man operation's charter," April said, coldly now, "is a full and open communication channel from you to Mack. It does not necessarily run the other way—Mack has carte blanche to operate in any way he sees fit, without consulting you or anyone else. If that does not seem fair, too bad. It is the only way Mack will have it in the first place, as you and the president well know. It works. And most important, you agreed to it. So don't start holding out now, Hal, or it might stop working."

"I realize all of that, April," Brognola said evenly. "You have my word. What I just told you did not develop until today." He respected this woman. She executed her authority with flair. She was successful in identifying problems and doing something about them. And she was in love with Mack Bolan.

"All right," the dark-haired beauty said, her voice still harsh. "I'll accept your word. Of course I believe you, Hal." She leaned back in her chair.

Sure, Brognola loved the guy, too, in his own way.

That's how it was when two large men put their lives on the line for each other. He knew, too, that when he looked into April's face, he saw pure loyalty—proud, fierce, utterly unwavering. All the loyalty the woman possessed was given over to that one man, because within him was embodied everything that April believed could be right with the world.

"There is—" Aaron glanced at the video display "—only a thirty-percent probability that any group in the sequence of forces is following up in Salmon River right now. The isolation of that country would not necessarily be in their favor. Still, thirty percent is thirty percent."

"All right," April said levelly. "That means there are three chances in ten that a highly trained force of professional assassins—numbers unknown—is fishing the Salmon River for Mack."

"Mack's vacation is still just that, April," Kurtzman continued gently, "and we must remember it. We don't have a chance in hell of finding him overnight with a force small enough to stay discreet. He is anywhere in a wilderness area of endless acreage. We'd be wasting our resources to send our own forces in when premature action would have to be overkill, and thus jeopardize Mack's own tactics. He's the one who's doing the surviving. He knows exactly where he is, and he knows how to survive. We must give him room to proceed his way—room in the sense of time, I mean. He already has the space out there. My counsel is that we will hear from him when he's ready.''

Hal Brognola looked toward April.

''If,'' said April, ''we have not heard from him by 1200 hours tomorrow morning....''

''We send in the marines,'' said Hal.

''I was thinking of Jack Grimaldi and Able Team.'' April smiled.

''Same thing,'' Kurtzman said, only half-kidding. Carl Lyons, Rosario ''Politician'' Blancanales and Herman ''Gadgets'' Schwarz—The Executioner's Able Team—along with pilot Jack Grimaldi, at home at the controls of everything from a hang glider to an F-16 fighter-bomber, continued to be an elite cadre that was the equal of several score ordinary soldiers of the line.

''We've sweated out twelve hours waiting for Mack before,'' Kurtzman said resignedly.

''We've sweated out a lifetime,'' April said. ''And it doesn't get easier.'' She looked ahead through soft dark eyes. She had been waiting for the man whom she loved ever since she had met him, living with fear for his life as her constant companion.

Hal smiled bravely. ''The odds say that Mack is having the time of his life.''

But Mack and Hell combined tended to twist the odds, just like death changes the shape of life. And they knew that.

They knew that Mack's sojourn in America's primal heartland was turning the wilderness into a caldron.

Hell was bubbling again. What would the fire-storm teach this time?

They waited in trepidation, keeping their counsel, in the thrall of that large man who beckons Hell to come forth and then dispatches it with such swiftness and strength and detachment.

It was a form of higher learning for the world, these demonstrations of what a man, one man, can do. The Stony Man War Room attended upon its un-folding, in anxiety and hopeful prayer.

11

Bolan was almost back to the Corey Bar campsite when he heard engine noise again. It was not the low-horsepower ratchet of the trail bikes but the lower, throatier thrum of a jet boat, carefully picking its way downstream in the darkness, through the treacherous streambed.

Back around the river bend toward the Guths' camp, Bolan could just make out the leading edge of a power searchlight. The boat's engine throttled down and the light swept out of sight. Someone said, "Put her in as close as you can, but watch out for the rocks."

Metal hull scraped gently against sand and granite, then Bolan heard the splash of people clambering ashore. Someone softly called the names of the bike crew as the shore party reconnoitered.

It would not take long to find what Bolan had left behind on the bar: three riderless bikes, two lifeless hulks.

Bolan moved on past the last rockfall, his black wet suit-clad figure invisible against the shadows. He made the campsite, crouching low.

Both kayaks, as well as Johnny Kerr, were gone.

"Johnny," Bolan called, his hushed voice only

loud enough to be heard over the water's rush and the jet boat's grumble.

"Over here."

The youth was standing in the shadow of a gnarled old cottonwood, unconcealed except by his absolute stillness. He was holding a straight branch long as he was tall, its end whittled to a sharp point. His young face was a hard mask of determination.

Bolan took a step toward him, and for a moment Johnny still did not move as his eyes drilled into the advancing black figure. He lowered the spear only when Bolan was near enough to be hit—and beyond mistaking.

"It's okay, Johnny," Bolan said, gentling the boy. "You're doing fine." Bolan moved forward quickly, taking the boy by the arm to nudge him back into the cottonwood's drooping foliage, easing him down into a crouch.

Johnny inclined his head upstream. "They've got another boat." His voice was unsteady. "What do we do?"

"For now we wait."

The jet boat's engine revved up, and a minute later it came around the calmer waters of the river bend and into their view. It was moving slowly. The three trail bikes were piled in the stern. The spotlight was mounted on gimbals on the deck of the bow, two men in rubber-soled shoes squatting on either side of it. They were dividing its time between scanning the river ahead for hazards and sweeping the banks for their prey.

"There," one of them snapped.

He was pointing directly at Bolan and Johnny.

The other guy swiveled the light around. The yellow oval of its beam slipped across the sand and on toward their position, until its perimeter was only inches from their feet.

Then the jet boat lurched, the light suddenly flashing upward.

"What the hell—"

"We hung up on a rock or something. Get that damn light back on the river!"

The boat lurched again as it slid off the boulder and settled back into the channel. In moments it was out of sight, altogether.

Close beside Bolan, Johnny began to breathe again.

"What happened back at the Guth cabin?" he whispered.

Bolan told him, without holding anything back. He did not want Johnny scared unnecessarily, but it was essential the boy understand the facts. The deadly facts.

Men were trying to kill them.

Johnny stared down at the ground. He picked up a handful of sand, ground fine as cornmeal by the river over the aeons, and let it sift through his fingers. "Mack," he said quietly, not looking up.

Bolan waited. It was important that the youth talk now.

Because he would have to act soon enough.

"I guess I know my way about these parts pretty well," Johnny said slowly, weighing each word to ensure that it would convey exactly what he meant.

"I've been over this country in canoes and kayaks and rafts, on horseback and foot. In a way I've made it mine. I'm somewhat prideful of that."

"A man should be proud of his accomplishments," Bolan told the boy—and thought again of his own brother, and of his progress into manhood.

"I know how to take care of myself," Johnny continued. "I've been run up a tree by a black bear. I've come close as I am to you to being rattlesnake-bit. But I never had nothing to do with men trying to kill other men. What the hell do they want, Mack? Are you some kind of secret agent or something?"

"Or something," Bolan said lightly. "What counts now is getting you out of here in one piece."

"No," Johnny said firmly. "What counts is making sure those men don't ever bother anyone again." The youth sifted another handful of sand. "In a couple, three days my pa will be out of the hospital, and he and mom will come back to Salmon River, just like always. But things won't be the same ever again, whether they know it or not. There'll always be the chance those men will come back. Next week, or next year. I'd live the rest of my life looking over my shoulder. We must stop them now."

"They'll be stopped, Johnny," Bolan said. "You have my word on that."

"I reckon it's up to us," Johnny said. "Unless you've got some reinforcements stashed in that rabbit brush yonder." He was trying for a light tone and he halfway made it.

Downriver the sound of the jet boat faded into the water's rush. There was nothing about this situation that Bolan liked. The boy was a bystander, a non-combatant. His safety had to come first.

Yet the interdiction and termination of Vigoury and his hit team was also primary. He was the terrorist secret weapon, the true killing machine. Bolan had located the name in his mental file, had recalled the chilling information gleaned from the Frank Edwards operation. If Vigoury were allowed to succeed here on Salmon River, the terrorist network would be that much stronger, that much more confident.

And as near as Bolan could figure it, the two goals—Johnny's salvation, Vigoury's extermination—were inextricably tied.

The winding land trail back to Corn Creek was twenty-five miles of steep switchbacks and ankle-twisting drops. It could not possibly be covered in less than eight hours, hours in which Mack and his new, young brother in blood would be without cover or mobility.

Bolan the soldier had learned to pick the time and place for combat whenever he could. Maybe even here, within the river canyon's containment, it was possible.

The first step was to even up the sides a little.

It was back to the jungle. Like in Vietnam, he would make this new battle one of attrition. The combat plan would be to relentlessly blast the enemy. Hit after hit. No more containment. Now it was war.

The kayaks and supplies were behind the cottonwood in a little runoff gully. "Feel up to some kayaking?" Bolan asked.

Johnny gave him a grin and stood. "You bet."

"Only on the river can we outmaneuver them," Bolan explained as he carried his boat across the bar. "They won't be able to hear us, but we'll hear their engine."

"Unless they use a raft," Johnny pointed out.

"What's the river like downstream?"

"It's tough and it's big," Johnny said. "Salmon Falls has been dynamited out a couple of times over the years, and that broke up some of the rocks and evened out the drop a mite. Also it's partly washed out in water this high, but it's still plenty gnarly. And once you get through, it doesn't get any easier. There's a lot of white water below us."

Bolan glanced at the sky. "We'll have the moonlight for a while. We'll have to be real sharp every foot of the river. But we'll make it."

Bolan looked directly at the rugged boy-man standing beside his kayak, waiting and ready.

"There are going to be times when keeping real sharp takes an extra effort, an extra skill," he told the youth. "So when I give an order, you follow it. No questions, no hesitation. Understand?"

"Yes."

Johnny held out his hand, and Bolan took it, felt the strength and conviction in the grip. He contained as much as he could the deep agony within him, the wrenching pain of his knowledge of this boy's destiny. His feelings were choking him up inside.

Bolan turned away abruptly. "Let's move out, brother John," he said gruffly. He picked up his kayak and went down to the dark water.

12

They took the far-right channel through the falls, shooting through the raging white water as silent as the night. Bolan was in the lead, helmeted and skirted up, and he set a steady pace: the paddle windmilling in his strong hands, the concave blades taking even bites at the swirling water.

On the left bank steam rose into the chill night air from Barth Hot Springs, where water at a steady 134 degrees year-round gurgled out of a rock seep to mingle with the river, a hundred degrees cooler. Not far past the springs, the river's roar rose.

"Bear Creek on the right," Johnny called, paddling up beside Bolan. The two kayakers back-paddled, holding steady against the current. "Just past is Hancock Rapids, runnin' the better part of a mile. I'd better lead us through."

They had covered several miles in the hour since they had left Corey Creek, and over the stretch Bolan's combat sense had been honed to high readiness. "Stay close," he said now, "but let me keep the lead."

Johnny may have had more experience spotting the river, but Bolan had more experience spotting killers—before they spotted him.

"Look for the vee on the left," Johnny called, "then stick to the channel. But watch out for fast water. There are some incredible whirlpools near the far end."

Bolan pointed his bow into the upcoming cleft and felt the current grab the Mirage and accelerate it. Ahead he could see the foaming white water of the Class Three rapids. He did not fully anticipate their force until he was in them. They were bigger than anything he had seen so far. Standing waves five feet high loomed above him, silvery in the moonlight, poised for a moment before pounding down on the bow of the Mirage as it sliced a path through. A rock cut the water to the left, and when Bolan braced to shoot around it, he overcompensated and felt the boat begin to dump. He went with the motion, setting his paddle as he rolled.

Underwater he had a strange, dazzling impression of the streambed as the moonlight filtered through to it. It looked like an alien landscape. As he continued to hang upside down, rocks rushed by all around him. Some were only inches from his helmeted head. Bolan swept with the long paddle—and felt the blade cut cleanly through without giving him any leverage with which to right himself.

The roiling white water was so aerated it was too thin to provide sufficient resistance.

Bolan's air started to give out.

He braced and swept again, this time digging more deeply, reaching for the current.

A sharp pointed rock rising three feet from the bottom rushed at his face.

Bolan pulled hard, snapped his hips sideways.

The rock swept away somewhere beneath him as his torso burst through the surface, cool fresh air coursing into his opened throat.

"Mack," Johnny called out. "You all right there?"

Bolan flashed a thumbs up. He was better than all right now. Adrenaline coursed warm through his bloodstream.

That was when he saw the two guys on the cable car.

The cable crossed the river maybe four hundred yards ahead, a single strand of braided steel suspended from tripods of yellow pine anchored on either bank.

A car on pulleys rode the cable, run by hand-over-hand power. It was the work of some long-ago prospector who needed year-round access to his claim; the Forest Service had no doubt maintained it to connect up with a hiking trail.

Now, evidently, it had been converted into a goddamned gunnery mount.

Two guys were crouched precariously on the car's platform, clutching submachine guns to their sides and scanning upstream. The swollen river ran only four feet beneath them.

"Johnny," Bolan cautioned softly.

All hell broke loose.

One of the chatterguns spoke, the muzzle flash like the flicker of an old silent movie. Slugs splattered into the water immediately in front of Bolan. He drew hard to the right, throwing his body forward as he stroked.

"Hit the shore," he shouted behind him. "Then stay put."

Another burst sputtered out from the cable car, this time directed at the boy. From the edge of his vision Bolan saw Johnny throw his body left and dump into a roll. When he came up again, he was shielded behind a cabin-sized boulder.

By then Bolan was fifty yards downstream.

His purpose had been to draw fire away from the youth. But he was now into the rapids, and he was committed.

The only way out was under that cable car.

He stayed low, exploiting to the maximum the maneuverability of the streamlined Mirage, ruddering and using the Duffek brace to turn the downriver hurder into a broken-field run. Hot lead hissed into the water a foot to the right of his bow. Bolan leaned and stroked hard on the opposite side, cornering clean as an Indy racer.

The firing twice stopped momentarily as each gunner changed clips. Bolan used the pauses to slip cross-channel right in front of the shooters, to reach the left-bank cliff-face, where he would brace downstream and move into his concealment. From the cable car one of the men said, "Now where the hell...?"

The cliff ran out, and he was in open water again.

No more than two boat-lengths ahead the river crashed over a rock eddy and dropped a full two feet. Fifty yards beyond that, the two gunmen on their precarious perch drew a dead bead on their target.

Bolan propelled the Mirage directly over one of the

water-smoothed boulders. The speckled face of the rock passed inches below his keel.

He plunged into the suckhole on the other side.

It was three feet wide and easily as deep. The bow of the Mirage arrowed into it and for a moment the boat was vertical, its rear end completely out of the water.

Bolan gasped his lungs full of oxygen before the hole swallowed up him and the boat.

As he had planned.

The swirling, powerful hydraulic held him and the Mirage underwater, despite the flotation vest and the boat's airbags. The only way up to the surface—was down.

The face of the speckled rock was close enough to touch. Water cascaded over it to pound down on Bolan.

He pulled up on the release loop of the spray skirt's shock cord and the skirt came loose of the coaming. Holding the paddle in one hand and the boat in the other, Bolan pushed free, his head breaking icy water only for a moment, too fast for a breath, before the hole pulled him under and horizontal again.

Bracing his feet against the boulder, Bolan shoved the boat toward the bottom, then swam hard after it, his lungs straining against the exertion and oxygen deprivation.

The undercurrent caught the boat, and it shot out of Bolan's hands. Out of the hole's grip, it rose toward the surface.

But the hydraulic was pulling Bolan back into its airless hold.

Bolan stroked again, using the still-held paddle for leverage. For a moment his body was the rope in a life-or-death tug-of-war between icy hole and frigid undercurrent.

Bolan added his waning strength on the undercurrent's side, and the hole gave up the fight.

He shot to the surface. He drew in deep ragged breaths. He did not stroke, but let the swift rapids hurl him downstream. In the black wet suit he was virtually invisible among the dark waves that carried him on.

One of the men on the cable car called out, "He got dumped into the drink."

"He's been under almost two minutes. He's a goner."

Bolan was ten yards away and closing on an underwater trajectory that would pass directly under them.

"Drowned like a rat," one of the guys said.

Bolan extended the paddle before him, held one blade with both hands.

As he was swept like streamlined flotsam beneath the cable, Bolan shot the paddle straight up in the air above him. It was the submarine launch of an improvised but powerful catch pole. The high blade hooked the cable car.

Bolan kept a tight grip on the upright paddle, and the car's platform tilted forward at a crazy angle as Bolan hurtled beneath it, the current's strength added to his own.

Two screams of terror split the Idaho night.

One of the gunmen belly flopped into the killing water, arms and legs thrashing, the guy berserk with panic. He tried to call for help and never got past the first syllable when water gushed into his stomach and lungs, speeding him toward chill death. He was no longer thrashing when he sped past Bolan, who was equipped in attire to stay submerged and active against the current.

The other guy had hold of the edge of the car, so he managed to prolong his agony. From the knees down, his legs hung in the water, the river tugging insistently against his grip on the platform's cold metal.

Bolan stroked back with huge strength and swung the paddle into the guy's gut.

The gunner howled, folded up, let go and hurtled past Bolan. He kept on howling for maybe thirty seconds, then the howling ended.

Bolan let the current take him again. Even with the wet suit the water was a chill, black presence all around him, and for a moment he heard the death howl's shrill ghost-echo, and the big guy himself felt his own human vulnerability.

There was something truly awful in the river's strength, a cosmic natural power that dwarfed man and all his technologies.

The Mirage was bobbing cockpit down in a back eddy. Bolan crawled through the current to it, still holding the paddle as an extension of his arm until he reached the kayak and dragged it and himself out on the rock. Lifting one end at a time so the water's weight would not buckle the hull, he emptied it. He was breathing hard.

Johnny was paddling toward his position.

Bolan had made the river his ally, just as in Vietnam the jungle had been at various times his cover, his billet and his sustenance.

It was another way he and Johnny Kerr were alike, Bolan realized. The darkness of night, the ruggedness of the country, and swiftness and strength of the cold, deep river were all silent partners to his good fight, allies to those who would ally with them.

Soldiers of the same side.

Bolan stood as Johnny docked in among the rocks.

The river's got ways, Miss Poten had said.

Yeah.

The Executioner had ways as well.

13

It was a head party, like a relic of the Mafia campaigns. But instead of a sleek, black Cadillac limousine, this gang of guncocks was riding a black Hypalon raft.

There were a half-dozen of them, grim, dark, horribly similar-looking men cradling automatic weapons, scanning the river and the two banks. One of the guys was different, the one in the bow looking as if he were wearing a Halloween mask with protruding eyes. Night-vision goggles, Bolan noted, capable of amplifying the available moonlight five hundred times, turning the deepest shadow into day.

They'd need more than goggles, Bolan thought grimly.

Seeing was one thing. Believing was another.

Bolan was about to turn them into believers.

The raft was a big Sport II Expedition model, fully fifteen feet long, an outfitter's rig built of the highest quality materials and designed to handle the biggest rapids. An aluminum-tubing frame with a molded plastic pilot's seat was mounted between the two inflated thwarts, dark paddles that swung out from swivel locks.

The oarsman looked as though he knew at least

something about rowing and river-running. He kept the boat well headed in the racing water, using the oars to steer and pull through the riffles, rowing without wasted motion. Two gunnies flanked the guy in the night-goggles in the bow, and another pair manned the stern, sweeping the backtrack with their submachine guns.

The two hunted kayakers were ten miles downstream from the cable car, and by Bolan's chronometer it was nearing midnight. They had disembarked and were onshore. The rapids at this point were known as Big Mallard, directly down from the natural fortification Bolan had chosen in the rocks. Though one of the few Class Four rapids on Salmon River, Mallard was usually washed out in water this high.

Usually. Instead it was a raging torrent, tons of water foaming in front of the hidden warriors and boiling over two high rock falls. Jagged stone reached into the night sky as if in supplication. Standing waves were tall as a man; they thrashed above hungry gaping suckholes. The roar was as loud as an express train.

"I've seen this happen once or twice," Johnny whispered. "It's one of the reasons you can never really know the river. There's a landslide or an avalanche, or a sandbar builds up where there was never one before, and all of a sudden a little riffle turns into a boat-chewing rapid. Like this." He nodded toward the water. "Mallard was big before. But Jeez. . . ."

The head party was nearing them at the lip of the

white water, the raft beginning to pick up speed.

"They'll never make it," Johnny breathed.

Not if Bolan had anything to do with it.

From inside the wet-suit jacket he took the lethal little Ingram M-11 he had liberated from the dead biker above Corey Bar. He rechecked the 32-round magazine, pulled back the cocking handle and gave it a quarter turn to set the safety on "off."

The big terrorist raft swept into the rapids' head-waters.

"Watch out for the goddamn rocks!" someone hollered.

"It's rock proof, asshole," the leader yelled, straining to keep the craft properly headed.

Bulletproof, *too*? Bolan muttered to himself.

The raft hung for a moment on the first ledge, then plunged crazily over.

A huge spray of white water completely engulfed the front half of the boat, and for a moment it seemed to stand on its nose. Men cried out as they were tossed around like pinballs, grabbing at the painters running along the gunwales. Then the tail end of the boat slapped back, and it was more or less on an even keel again. The steersman was good all right; Bolan had to give him that. The guy pulled hard on the right oar, and the boat headed and swirled into the miasma.

Then the moment of fake calm was past, the boat whirled on, bucking through standing waves like a sunfishing bronco, slipping over rock falls, barely missing slurping holes. In bow and stern hardguys had been thrown together in a jumble of arms and legs and guns. Now they grabbed each other and the boat in their efforts to untangle themselves and get back upright.

The one in the night-vision goggles had given up his surveillance of the banks in favor of avoiding being tossed into the racing water. The boat was approaching the second ledge.

Bolan and Johnny held back their position.

"They'll never make it over that weir," Johnny murmured. "They'll flip that thing for sure."

Bolan rested both forearms on a chest-high rock, spread his legs. The Ingram was wrapped in his right fist. His left supported the short barrel.

The terrorists' boat hung above the ledge as if trying to make up its mind whether to commit itself.

Bolan gave it a shove.

Flame from the Ingram's muzzle spat a 16-round burst of .380 tumblers that stitched the raft from bow to stern. The synthetic rubber Hypalon was quality material all right, but no, it was not bulletproof.

Neither were the gunners of this head party.

The steering oarsman was flopped over the left gunwale so that the weight of his body helped to rapidly force air out through the neat row of bullet holes that decorated the craft's side. Bolan had hit about three of the six separate air chambers, but three would be plenty.

Comprehension of what had come down dawned on the other five men, as revealed by their sudden chorus of panic.

They were sinking in the midst of the most deadly rapids on the River of No Return.

The boat coursed over the ledge, listing hard to its crippled left side, mere degrees away from fulfilling Johnny's prediction by flipping. The guy in the night-vision goggles tumbled out into one of the holes below the ledge and disappeared.

The lopsided raft spun out of control.

The starboard oar caught against a rock and swung around, cold-cocking one of the stern men. His partner ducked and lunged for the oar's handle—and missed.

His momentum carried him over the side, but he managed to hang on to a fistful of deflated Hypalon. One of the bowmen screamed, "Let go, you goddamn son of a...."

The raft flipped.

The unconscious guy's horror was over; he slipped below the surface immediately. Another guy managed to claw his way up to air—a moment before the current slammed him headfirst into a rock. It made a sound like a watermelon hitting the sidewalk from a great height.

The third guy saw what happened to his buddy and got smart. Arms pumping like pistons, he turned himself around, feet pointing downstream, just in time to hit the deadly rock with the soles of his hiking boots. He was able to momentarily stop himself as the current parted around him.

He should have got a little smarter.

The half-deflated raft swept over him like something ugly and black from a monster movie, one hundred and forty pounds of thick wet rubberized material suffocating him and dragging him down.

The raft bucked once, as if burping after the meal it had just ingested, and then swept on past the rock, leaving nothing in its wake.

Somehow the last member of the head party had gotten out of the channel. He was swimming for all his might in a fear-crazed Australian crawl, fighting to reach the eddy line, momentarily warmed by his fear. In one desperate effort he lurched half out of the water, and then he was into the calm along the rocky bank. He got boots to river bottom, stood, staggered, fell to his knees. He had to crawl the last few feet to shore.

There he knelt on all fours, his head down.

Bolan stroked the Ingram's trigger, and a single .380 mangler cored into the bridge of the guy's nose, the muzzle energy of the weapon punching the guy half-erect and back into the water. For the range was a mere two feet.

What had been the near guy's face was a featureless mask of white-flecked red gore as he slipped back into the river's icy bosom.

"Oh, Jeez," Johnny moaned behind him. The boy's eyes were wide and his mouth open as he stared at the place where the guy had been.

"Get the boats, Johnny."

"Jeez...."

"Get the boats." Bolan made his voice harsh, insistent. He had to keep the boy moving, keep him from dwelling on the terrifying vision just witnessed.

Johnny shivered, then moved back into the rocks where the kayaks were cached.

Terror was the vicious thing beyond all other things that savages reveled in, raining upon all those weaker than themselves.

Now the Executioner sowed that same terror where it would reap the greatest good.

14

If Bolan had had any compunction about taking out the guy who almost made it ashore, it was assuaged the second he fired because he had caught a glimpse of the hardboy's face. In the simultaneous time it took for synapses to complete the mental circuit, Bolan matched the face against the mug file in his head and came up with a name and a connection.

The name was Pete Magnini.

There was nothing clean about Pete Magnini, despite Vigoury's opinion that no arrest record meant clean.

His job had been to take whatever steps were necessary to get his victims to toe the Mafia line. The victims were always the ordinary people, the sweetest of the streets, and the steps were tainted with the very worst violence, always escalating from threats through beatings to murder.

With the Mafia in shambles—thanks to the sustained fire of a certain blitzing warrior in midnight black—it was logical that Magnini would turn for employment to the latest manifestation of Animal Man: the network of international terrorism. Bolan was only too aware of the links between the remains of *La Cosa Nostra* and the ideological hate-mongers.

He had seen it in action when he scorched to smoldering ruins the "terrorist summit" of would-be czar Luke Harker in the Algerian Sahara. Further confirmation came in the Florida Everglades, when Bolan took apart the works of one Thurston Ward, business tycoon and megalomaniac.

Ironically, the Mafia itself had originally been a terrorist organization claiming to be a democratic people's movement pushing a political cause and an end to oppression.

The terrorist movement followed the Mafia model, but took an immediate shortcut. Ostensibly its actions and motivations were purely political. But what was political about a car-bomb parked in a residential neighborhood? About the ransom kidnapping of an American businesswoman in Cental America? About the assassination of a Turkish diplomat in broad daylight on a street in Ottawa, the capital of Canada.

The motivations of mafioso and terrorist alike were personal enrichment, wealth, power and the suffering of anyone who stood in their way.

Terrorism could only exist in a free society. That was why there was no terrorism in the Soviet Union—except what the state inflicted on its citizens. In a social system where everyone is required to carry identification papers and produce them on demand, where speaking one's mind is a felony, and where people can be imprisoned on the whim of the government, terrorism is already there. It is owned and operated by the government. Fascism buys bullies, it buys all the means of fear, and it uses them itself.

But in the United States and the democracies of the Free World, where freedoms of speech, movement and association are the bedrock of civil liberty, terrorism flourishes independent of all laws.

The terror-mongers run amok here. Unfettered by decency or humanity, and of course free of the preemptive existence of totalitarianism, armed with the latest weaponry and a disregard for any other person's life, a relatively small number of terrorists sow seeds of huge violence all around the world.

Until Mack Bolan pits his talents, his considerable talents, against them.

Suddenly, someone else as well is playing outside the rules.

BOLAN DECIDED it was time to take the gloves off.

He would speak some more in the language of death.

When the Executioner was finished here, there would be nothing left in Salmon River country of Vigoury and his gang but their stink.

Even that would go away in time.

15

The guard was watering a wild-rose bush, staring down at his stream, when Mack Bolan rose up behind him. Bolan slapped his left palm over the guy's nose and mouth to jerk back his head, at the same time driving the knife hilt-deep into his right kidney. He pulled the blade out again immediately, and the guy puffed a soft sigh into the restraint of Bolan's palm. Then the knife slashed from ear to ear in a swooping throat-opening coup de grace.

Bolan lowered the deadweight to the sand. Blood poured from the gaping wound and puddled all around him, mixing with the urine, all shiny black in the night's dimness.

In the previous hour he and Johnny had put more river behind them, along with the landslide-swollen rapids where the raftload of headhunters had taken their final swim. They had paddled with superior sportsmen's skill, going with the current's flow, saving their strength for what lay ahead. Bolan spent the time figuring probabilities.

Vigoury would have to improvise a hardsite. Standard Operating Procedure said that small hit teams had the advantages of mobility, easier concealment and flexibility. But the small groups had come up empty four times in a row, and Vigoury was down to half his original force. His best plan would be to mob up, blockade the river and figure that sooner or later Bolan and the boy would have to pass.

Bolan soon knew his hunch was confirmed.

The hit team had chosen the Rhett Creek Campground for a place to go hard. It was a fair-sized space in a grove of pine and quaking aspen against the foot of the steep canyon wall. There was a privy back from the water, a picnic table and a sloping sandy beach. The camping area was hardpan sand and scrub grass, framed with deadfall logs arranged to form three sides of a square and painted dark brown.

A half-dozen figures were strewed around the clearing, cocooned in sleeping bags.

A guy served as close security, sitting on the far-border log smoking, cupping his cigarette butt against the chill night breeze and taking quick shallow drags, his eyes constantly roving about the camp and the stretch of the river visible from his position.

Thirty men at the start, more or less, according to Johnny's estimate. Fifteen dead already—sixteen including the sentry Bolan had just consigned to the universe. Six men asleep here, one on nervous guard.

That left six or so men on the outside perimeter.

These became the ice-eyed nightguy's target.

He knew before he began—before he disembarked and launched his silent solo death stalk—that his targets would be scared, keyed-up with the tension of the night and their own dark apprehensions. They were out of their element, these guys, for they were savages of an urban jungle. The wilderness held only unnamed dread for them.

Mack Bolan moved through the darkness among the widely spaced perimeter guards.

Unlike those he stalked, he was brother to the forest, quiet and discreet, and he affirmed that brotherhood by eliminating those who invaded the forest, who violated the dark nature that afforded him protection.

He visited them one by one, and without noise or light or argument, he dispatched them. He laid the knifed carcasses on the forest floor and silently apologized to his fraternal force here for the indignity of that. As the terrorists' numbers grew weaker, the big guy grew stronger, and when he was finished the combat odds had been cut by half.

Below in the camp, the inside man lit another cigarette from the butt of his last.

Bolan passed behind the privy, which put him behind the guy and above him, maybe ten feet up a steep grade of loose rock. The guy's eyes were still darting on their perpetual quest, in every direction but Bolan's.

The nightknifer became the nightscorcher, checked the selector on the M-16 appropriated from his last victim and softly called, "Up here."

The guy's head snapped around—in time to take a 5.56mm bonecrusher in the face.

The single report tore apart the night's tranquillity. Heads popped up, fingers fumbled within the cramped quarters of mummy-cut sleeping bags, trying to undo zippers. Confused half-panicked men were jolted from the phantasmagoria of dreams into a terrible reality.

None was free of his sleeping bag when Bolan opened up from the vantage point above them.

He worked coldly, methodically. He did not clamp his finger around the trigger in a lead-spraying death grip, but instead placed controlled three-round bursts with excellent effect. A lumpy sleeping bag twitched and then lay still, clouds of goose down floating up out of bullet holes. A hardguy wildly tried to slap his two hands over the three blood geysers across his chest. Cold death stalked through the campsite.

Bolan fired and fired again. A guy tried to get out a handgun, but the hammer snagged on the sleeping bag's ripstop nylon, and a moment later he no longer needed the gun. Another guy managed to fire, and somewhere in the darkness lead whined in ricochet off rock. A swarm of 5.56mm tumblers took the guy away before the first echo had died, until the bolt of the M-16 locked open.

Bolan stood, senses stretched to the limit. Nothing moved except the night breeze and the river's inexorable flow.

Bolan went among the mangled bodies that littered the little stretch of sand, turning two of them on their backs, quick-scanning faces and figures. In a pack leaning against a log he found three loaded magazines for the M-16. He slipped them inside the wet suit.

Fourteen men.

Fourteen men where he was sure there should be more.

This war was far from over.

16

The tiny bar where Johnny Kerr was waiting was hidden between the trail and the river. As Bolan came back down into it, he called the prearranged password.

Johnny had lit the Coleman stove. He poured from a pot and handed a cup to Bolan as the big man in black sat with the M-16 near at hand. Johnny gazed at the rifle neutrally.

Bolan had expected coffee, but the cup was full of a rich, thick broth, complete with flavorful chips of reconstituted beef. As soon as the aroma hit his nostrils, Bolan's appetite switched on. He had trained himself to go without food for long periods when combat conditions demanded he do so. But the soup was damned well needed, and it was damned good.

"In the back country," Johnny said quietly, "food is as important as the right kind of clothing. You can't survive with either one of them alone. With the night temperature down near forty and the water colder than that, it takes a lot of calories just to keep the body functioning. If you throw in a lot of physical stuff—like paddling seventy miles of river in one night—you need even more."

Bolan accepted another cup of broth, gulped it down.

"A lot of people are talking about survival nowadays," Johnny said, working out his need to talk, "The way things are going in the world, I don't blame 'em. Having my kayak all outfitted and ready to go, that's part of it for me. If something happens—something big and very bad—I plan to be ready. Ready for when it happens, and ready to go on surviving when it's done and past."

He took a long drink of his soup. "People kind of watch out for number one. That's all right, I guess. I'm the same way, mostly. After... after something like a nuclear attack, there'll be those who aren't ready at all, maybe trying to take it away from those who are. That's not right, is it?"

Bolan gave him a gentle smile of encouragement.

"But I guess there's more to it than that," Johnny went on. "If we're going to have to start over, we have to be ready for that, too. Me surviving, that doesn't mean much. The country's got to survive, too."

It had taken strong and special men to build the American nation. If it were ever necessary to rebuild it, strong men would be needed once more—men like the one Johnny Kerr would grow to be.

"How are you holding up, young John?" Bolan asked.

Johnny offered a little foil-wrapped packet. "My own recipe," the youth said. "Honey, nuts, grains. Lots of calories and it's high in protein. And it'll last for years without going bad."

"It's good," Bolan said around a mouthful of the sweet concoction.

Johnny turned off the Coleman's flame, and for a few moments they sat facing each other, letting their eyes readjust to the dimness.

"I'm doing okay," Johnny said finally. He picked up a stick of driftwood and began to draw aimless patterns in the sand. "I...I heard all the shooting back there. For a few seconds, it sounded like an army. I...."

"Say it, John."

"I was scared," the boy blurted. "I wasn't scared when they started shooting at me up at the lodge, or during any of the rest of it, but I was real scared just then." The words came tumbling out. "I was so scared I couldn't move."

"Fear isn't bad, John," Bolan said. "It's nothing to be ashamed of."

"You don't understand." The boy's voice cracked. "I was scared for *you*."

The boy looked up, and the moonlight was reflected in the watery pools of his eyes. "I knew you were way, way outnumbered, and I heard the guns, and I thought they'd got you for sure. Me, I could have outrun 'em easy."

With a start, Bolan realized the boy was telling the literal truth. Johnny knew every square foot of the Salmon River, and every cliff and canyon and ridge and creek drainage for a hundred miles around. He knew the woods like a big-city kid knew the subway. Not only that, but he had been hunting all his life and was probably as stealthy as a mountain-man fur trapper—or as stealthy as Bolan himself. With the night for an ally, Johnny would have been nearly invisible and soundless, and the chance of Vigoury's men catching him would have been nil.

"I never had a brother," Johnny said. "Me and pa are close as tomorrow, we do everything together and all—but it isn't the same."

Bolan knew what the boy felt. Mack Bolan did have a brother once—and had consciously and willfully put Johnny Bolan out of his life. Loneliness and the Executioner were no strangers.

"A guy needs a friend who's like himself." There was a plea in John Kerr's voice. "You know, someone he can talk to and learn things from. A guy he can look up to."

There was a tight lump in Bolan's throat as a picture of another young Johnny came to his mind's eye.

"I guess you must have lots of friends," Johnny said. Bolan smiled grimly to himself; friendship was a rare and precious commodity in the Executioner's life.

"But when this is over," Johnny went on, "maybe you and me. . .maybe we could see each other again, or maybe just write or talk or something."

"Maybe we could, Johnny," Mack Bolan said, and his voice was choked with long-denied emotion. "Maybe we could, brother John."

"Why do you call me that?"

"Because if I did have a brother," Bolan said, "I'd want him to be like you."

Johnny threw the stick over the rocks where it

splashed into the steam. "Back there at the camp—
did you . . .? I mean, were all of them—?"

Bolan told the boy of the body count, and of the
probability of Vigoury's survival farther downstream. "That's why I want you to get moving as
soon as we break camp."

"Get moving? Where?"

"Away from here. I should have realized before
that you could make it out anytime you wanted to. I
can't risk going after these guys with you along,
Johnny."

"You can't risk it without me," the boy said in a
man's voice. "This is my fight, too." His voice
softened. "I don't know who these men are. Heck,
Mack, I don't even know who you are, except you're
on the right side. All I know is they want to kill you—
and they tried to kill me. I'll take orders. You're the
boss. But I won't go back, not now. I've earned the
right."

Others had earned the right to join Bolan's fight
and had taken that right to the grave with them.
Johnny Kerr was hardly past boyhood.

But inside the boy was the heart of a man.

And yeah, he *had* earned the right.

Bolan rose, the decision made.

But he knew that if Johnny Kerr did not come
through this last long river-run, his blood would
forever stain Mack Bolan's soul, and Mack would
not choose to live on earth anymore.

17

"See where the channel sweeps way around to the left?"

Bolan followed the direction of Johnny's paddle and could just make out the bend in the river, maybe a half-mile ahead. The moon was sitting on the canyon's high ridge now; within minutes it would set.

"I see it," Bolan said.

"Jackson Bar is just past the bend, and that's where the road starts. If you're right—if they have more men after us—that's where we could figure to run into them."

"How do you see it, John?" Bolan back-paddled to stay abreast of the youth. The Mirage and Johnny's boat rode the eddy line a few yards out from shore, the Rhett Creek hardsite and the carnage an hour behind them.

"This is one of the few places in the seventy-five-mile run where you have outside access to the canyon," Johnny said. "And there are three different ways in. First is the road. It runs along the river for two, two and a half miles, but that's just a spur. The main road goes due north out of the canyon, up over the ridge and on to Elk City. It's gravel and pretty rugged this time of the year, but you wouldn't have any trouble in a four-wheel drive.

"Second, a little farther downstream the South Fork flows in. It's almost as difficult as this river in high water, so it's not as likely they'd come that way, but it is possible.

"Third, there's the airstrip. It's by a big old log lodge called Mackay Bar. There's hunting, fishing, boating, pack trips out of the lodge. You'll see a pack bridge hanging across the river. A lot of the dudes from the East don't have a lot of time to spend when they're here, and they want to get in and out as quick as they can. Still, it galls me sometimes, having to listen to airplanes setting down in the canyon."

"Is there anyone at the lodge now?"

"Chances are, no."

That was for the best. Innocent bystanders would be more hindrance than help at this point. "What else should I watch for, Johnny?"

"After we round the bend you can see the road, look for the Mackay Bar Campground on the right bank. Just past it, the river straightens for about a mile. Ludwig Rapids is at the head of the straightaway, and the white water will be plenty big. The pack bridge is at the end of the run, the airstrip on the left below it and the lodge on the left above. After that the road ends and the South Fork comes into the river. If we get that far we're home free."

Somewhere in the twenty miles remaining before civilization intruded on the River of No Return, an unknown number of men awaited them. The terror merchants had been defeated several times during this long night, and they would be especially cautious now, less likely to split their force, more determined than ever to win the deadly cat-and-mouse game.

They wanted Mack Bolan's head mounted on a sharp stick.

When they tried to take it, he would be ready.

Bolan had fieldstripped and cleaned the M-16 before reloading and stashing it in a spare waterproof sack. The bundle lay in the kayak's bow against the length of his right leg.

Nestled between his knees, in waterproof wrapping, was the spare tank of white gas for Johnny Kerr's Coleman stove. A greasy rag was stuffed tightly into the small opening at the top.

In its normal configuration, the high-efficiency little stove supplied heat nearly as high and concentrated as a blowtorch. In the jerry-rigged configuration Bolan had devised, the ten-ounce can became an incendiary grenade that would scatter boiling fire and jagged shrapnel.

Red digits glowing on Bolan's chronometer indicated it was nearing 0300. The moon was gone, and some clouds had drifted in to partially obscure the star field.

"Are you ready, young John?"

"Yes, sir," the youth said crisply.

"Stay close," Bolan reminded him. "And when I say go, you go—double-quick."

"I won't let you down, Mack."

"I know you won't, John." He took up his paddle. "Move out."

Around the first bend Johnny pointed to the roadway on the right. They cut back into the second half of the S-curve, and the canyon walls were dark and silent, except for the rising roar of Ludwig Rapids ahead. Bolan saw Mackay Bar Campground off the right channel where the ledge dropped off, a couple of hundred yards ahead.

Then another sound—rumbling, mechanical, alien to the dark wilderness—mixed with the rapids' roar and rose to dominate it.

Like some kind of futuristic beast devolved to exist alone of its species, the prow of the jet boat appeared above the ledge.

The pilot was babying the engine, taking his time and care going upstream over the treacherous half-visible rocks, the searchlight mounted on the bow surveying the water directly before it. The guy aiming it called back directions.

The boat moved forward in lurches as it climbed the foaming water ledges. For a moment the jet spouts were above the surface, and the boat's noise whined in higher pitch before the water jets settled under once more.

Steady in the channel, the boat picked up to a swifter headway. The spotlight man began to sweep the water and the banks on either side in a regular grid that would miss nothing.

The boat was one hundred yards off Bolan's bow and closing.

"Johnny," he said, soft and urgent. "Get to shore and dig in where you can hide the boat. Move."

"Mack...."

"Move!"

The searchlight swept Bolan's bow. Someone on the boat raised his voice in excitement.

Bolan jerked the shock cord of his spray skirt and

the rubberized fabric snapped free. He pulled the M-16 smoothly out of the kayak's bowels, stripped off the waterproof wrap, pulled back the charging handle. The small but lethal Coleman tank he jammed inside the wet-suit jacket.

He just had time to refasten the skirt when the searchlight locked onto him.

Bolan thumbed the selector, fired a single shot into the blinding glare. Glass exploded in a jagged shower and darkness returned to the river.

The engine's roar deepened, and the jet boat sat back on its stern as it picked up speed.

The boat was on a collision course with him, a ton of motorized metal hurtling down on Bolan at a closure rate of thirty miles per hour.

ETA: three seconds.

Bolan flicked the lighter, and the rag in the Coleman tank sputtered and flared. He cocked his arm.

If he missed there would be no second chance.

The boat's bulk ballooned before him, and then it was directly on him, blotting out all other existence with its roaring presence, and Bolan let the burning tank fly.

Then he stashed the M-16, sucked in air and rolled.

The jet boat's hull passed over him, the flying metal grazing the Mirage's tough underbody without doing damage. The blast of the water jets hit the Mirage and Bolan bobbed upside down, unscathed.

Through the water's damping he heard the first explosion.

Then the boat's tanks blew.

The sound and the shock wave combined to slam

into Bolan like an oak door, only force of will en-
abling him to retain what air was still in his lungs.
Debris splashed into the water all around him—
jagged pieces of superheated boat metal, charred
shapeless pieces of what had been human beings.

Bolan had been under at least a minute, and he
stayed under ten beats more. He set his paddle quickly but with exquisite care. He had neither the air nor
stamina for more than one attempted roll. Muscles
tensed in reflex, and he swept.

And popped upright into cold air.

The wilderness canyon looked like the set of a sur-
realist movie.

A movie set in Hell.

Curtains of steam drifted across the river, adding
to the eerie effect. Through it, and fifty yards upriver
from Bolan, was the jet boat's blackened hull, a
metal bowl of raging flame sending thick oily smoke
into the black air.

Floating debris covered the choppy surface all
around the death ship: bits of clothing, bright-
colored lifejacket panels, arms, legs, blackened
torsos.

The fire's light pushed back the darkness with
garish tongues of illumination that lapped at the
shadows of the canyon walls. Beyond the floating
torch of the crippled jet boat, Bolan got a glimpse of
Johnny Kerr. The boy had not made shore yet. In
fact he was stroking tentatively in Bolan's direction,
peering anxiously through the obscuring steam.

Bolan swung his paddle over his head, and Johnny
ruddered to a sliding stop and returned the signal.

Bolan rested the paddle across the Mirage's deck and held up both hands, palms out, in a "go back" sign.

He did not have a chance to see if Johnny obeyed.

If Bolan had not been pulling the Mirage around with a radical C-stroke, the short burst of autofire would have cut the boat—and the boater—in two. As it was, Bolan felt one of the slugs nip at the end of the right-hand paddle blade.

He tore back the spray skirt and redrew the M-16, the afterimage of the muzzle flash onshore still imprinted on his mind. A man-shape emerged from that position to separate itself from the deeper shadow of the rocks.

Bolan sent an eight-round burst of enlightenment among the veils of the Idaho night, and the man-figure rejoined the rocks. The Mirage bobbed violently against the recoil. Bolan braced his knees and counterbalanced, and the sleek craft rode it out.

Fifty yards farther downstream, another gunner opened fire, but the range, the night breeze and darkness conspired to send his burst ten feet wide of the mark.

Instead of returning lead, Bolan stroked hard for the bank.

On the other side, opposite the first gunman, yet another tried to track onto Bolan.

They had set up a gauntlet, a double line of armed men on both banks, a deadly cross fire arranged to turn the stretch of water before Bolan into a run for his life.

Bolan's element of surprise, a constant in his battle plays, was running out like the last quarter-inch of hourglass sand. The rifle-fire had told every gunner that the quarry had entered the gauntlet. When he did not show, they would know he had gone EVA, and they would mob up again.

Only the mob would be smaller than when it started.

Invisible in the waters, silent in the roar, Bolan lifted the Mirage from the river's edge and laid it among the rocks. The road was on a bench above the high-water line, open and exposed. Bolan moved down the shoreline instead, the Wet Shoes' rubber treads sure and silent on the slippery river-smoothed rocks.

The first gunner was crouched behind the redan of a three-foot block, his rifle resting on it with the barrel extending beyond. Bolan crept beneath him and set his back to the rock, bracing. Then his hands shot up and grabbed the gun barrel in both hands and pulled, hard as he could. The guy gave a grunt of surprise and came hurtling over Bolan to splat into the shallows on his back. Bolan wrenched the rifle loose of his grip. He dropped to his knees in the water and laid the barrel across the guy's throat, leaning all his weight on it. The crack of neck bone and the gurgle of the guy's death rattle sounded simultaneously.

Bolan was another fifty feet downstream, withdrawing the Buck knife from a guncock's bowels, when one of his buddies across the river called, "Hey, where is he? He shoulda been here by now."

Bolan set the M-16 on single shot. "Time to die," he called, loud enough to be heard above the noise of Ludwig Rapids.

Across the river a guy peered out of cover and said, "Is that you? Do you see the bastard?"

"I *am* the bastard," Bolan said, and sent a shot over the waves to punch through the gunner's skull.

Then right on schedule, the numbers ran out.

From the direction of the Mackay Bar Campground just down the road, men started shouting. "That was him, goddammit. He's on the shore."

"Mob up and move out," a voice of authority ordered. "There isn't fifty feet between the water and the canyon. Half of that is road. He's run out of territory. We've got him pinned."

Technically true, Bolan noted—as he moved on to secure further beachfronts.

He took up position on the campground's perimeter, camouflaged in a stand of willows. A dozen men occupied the little clearing and behind them, at the foot of the road that ran north to Elk City, were a couple of four-wheel-drive vehicles.

Bolan replaced the partially expended magazine with a full 30-round clip, acquired a target and began his cold methodical assault. Three-round bursts tore out of the darkness to find hit-man flesh, and bodies began to fall with clockwork regularity.

The fourth guy was down when the grenade arced through the air.

Bolan dived and rolled, finding rocky cover as the HE charge blew a hole in the night's fabric. Shrapnel whined by on either side of Bolan's protection. He was out and moving while metal was still splashing into the river.

He knee-and-elbowed across the depression of the

campground's sandy beach, coming up behind the remnants of the main assault force. Men were hunkered down behind logs, picnic tables, whatever improvised cover the campsite offered.

Bolan shot three terrorists in the back and was long-legging through his created battlefield while the others were still reacting. Panic searched out his position as he made the nearest vehicle. Someone howled, shot by one of his own men.

Bolan hurdled into the Jeep and twisted the key. The engine grated and then rumbled reluctantly to life. Bolan switched on the headlights, flicked the selector to high beam. Blinding glare slashed across the clearing, searing into eyes dilated by darkness.

Bolan floored the vehicle, cutting the wheel to send it into a sliding skid in the soft sand. For a millisecond the headlights froze the close-up of a fear-crazed face, and then something fragilely human thunked off the fender. The right side of the rig lifted and settled, and a tire rolled over the guy's middle.

Steering with his right hand, Bolan braced the M-16 out the window. In the yielding river-worn sand, the Jeep skewed around like a berserk bumper-car. Headlights swept across targets, followed a millisecond later by flesh-shredding lead.

Bolan braked hard enough to lock all four wheels and the Jeep slewed to a complete stop. In the back he found a crate with more grenades. He tossed it out into the sand, then pulled the rig to the other side of the clearing.

Two guys came out of darkness. Bolan rolled out of the vehicle as gunfire shattered the windshield. He came up from behind the door—came up firing and the two guys punched back into the darkness. Permanent darkness, here in America. A firefight in the New World. The frontier was alive again, with death.

The momentary silence was intense after the pandemonium of the firefight. But Bolan knew that every cross fire has two sides.

He utilized two of the grenades on the 4WD rigs, sprinting down the road as body metal and gasoline-hungry flames plumed into the night behind him.

The pack bridge was at the end of the road's dead-end spur, a one lane side-railed suspension affair swaying gently in the night breeze. On the other side, bulldozed into a flat landfill bench, was the airstrip.

Parked on it, at the foot of the sagebrush dotted slope, was a big transport helicopter, unidentifiable in the darkness, its rotor idling in a lazy circle. This was one hell of an assassination attempt. This was a major event. This was the hit-team nightmare Bolan had been waiting for since the day he first arose from the ashes as Colonel John Phoenix, counterterror topgun.

A dozen more men, the other half of the reinforcement squadron, was trotting single file toward the bridge, rifles at the port. They mobbed up at the bridge to sprint across in turn, exposing themselves only one at a time.

Bolan let the first guy make it.

But when the second guy started his move, Bolan lobbed the grenade.

The suspension bridge parted in the middle, the

two pieces flopping limply into the river. There was no sign of the guy on it; he might as well have been vaporized.

The killer ready to make the next dash had committed the grave error of taking a few steps out. Now he was hanging on to the bridge's rail, five feet below the hands trying to reach him.

The current whip-snapped the free end of the section, and the guy lost his grip. He slid down, like laundry in a chute, to splash into the water's icy blackness.

The guy who had already reached the other side spun around, searching for cover. Bolan sent a burst of 5.56mm tumblers to stitch him from gut to head. He tumbled back over the cut bank and disappeared.

The line of men across the river retreated toward the chopper as Bolan threw harassment fire across their path. A guy stumbled and went down, clutching at his leg. Someone grabbed him roughly under the arm and dragged him along the pavement, the guy screaming at what it cost his wounded limb. Rotors whirled as the men climbed desperately aboard, then the chopper lifted off, pivoted and ascended straight out of the canyon.

In a minute its raucous discord was consumed by nature's night sounds.

Bolan surveyed the battlefield. It was sobering to see how quickly man could desecrate what it had taken so long for the environment to create. Upstream, the jet boat was almost burned out, the sooty smoke of the smoldering remnants sending barely visible noxious black nimbi into the air. In front of

Bolan, battle flotsam swept through the rapids, as if someone had emptied his garbage pails into the crystal-pure water. Downstream to Bolan's right, the pack bridge, carefully crafted to blend into the natural setting, was now just kindling and warped steel cable.

But violation and desecration were the terrorist's marching orders. Professing to fight for a better world, he actually had little regard for any world. The terrorist lived not to create but to destroy. Nature and beauty meant nothing to those whose only concern was the technology of death.

The terrorscourger drew himself from the concealing darkness of his brothers, the forest and the night; he retook the road and trudged stolidly in the upstream direction. Then the long Mirage came into play again as Bolan reclaimed it and slid it into a launching eddy. As he used a series of draws and pries to ferry across the river, Bolan softly called out the boy's name.

River-rush and night sounds were all that he heard.

Bolan felt the dread grow within him as he paddled farther upstream, anxiously searching the shoreline, again calling out. He reversed, heading back down. There was a darker shadow among the rocks ahead.

Dread turned to raging anger as Bolan came up to the shadow.

The kayak was wedged between two rocks, impaled on the sharp tip of a third rock. A ragged gash in the fiberglass ran from cockpit to keel line.

There was no sign of Johnny Kerr.

18

The Precision Mirage shot down the River of No Return. Bolan's arms moved with the regularity of an automaton, the long paddle flashing through the air and trailing a slipstream of silvery droplets, the blades biting deeply into the channel. All of Bolan's upper-body strength was concentrated into a precise repetition of the forward stroke.

If he had divided his attention, Bolan might have been aware of the dull throbbing ache across his shoulder muscles, the leaden numbness of his arms. But all of his intentness was centered on the fate of Johnny Kerr.

To his right a stretch of granite cliffs two miles long loomed 500 feet high, the swiftest channel flowing right along their base. Bolan maneuvered into it with a draw and rudder, felt the power of the deep-flowing water added to his own desperate strength. Past the cliffs a series of man-made terraces climbed the opposite canyon slope, remnant of some long-abandoned mining operation.

The Mirage streaked silently past.

The rapids that remained were less difficult than those Bolan had already faced and overcome, but it would not have mattered either way. Salmon River was now only a moving highway, a necessary means to a precious end.

The torn kayak was a ruse, designed to confuse him or weaken his guard; Bolan was sure of that. Johnny was too good a riverman to have had that kind of accident. And even if he had somehow become disoriented or distracted by the firefight and wiped out, he would have been able to get safely out of the water, outfitted as he was with wet suit and PFD vest.

Johnny Kerr was not a victim of the River of No Return—but of the human vermin who recently infested it.

Indian Creek Campsite slid past on the right. Four miles farther on Bolan caught a glimpse of the Shepp Ranch outfitting cabin, and not long after, the larger Bull Creek Camp.

None showed any sign of human habitation.

Less than ten miles downriver was the beginning of the road to the town of Riggins. That marked the line between wilderness and civilization; several ranches and resorts lined the road.

So somewhere before their point, Vigoury was waiting.

Johnny Kerr by himself was of no worth to the terrorist hit-team leader, but he could be used: as a pawn, a hostage, a bargaining chip. As trade goods, redeemable in the surrender of the Executioner.

Again Mack Bolan thought of that other Johnny, his flesh-and-blood brother: forsaken for his own good, but still cherished in the gentle warrior's heart of hearts. With memory came a gut-wrenching sense of déjà vu.

This had all happened before, in another place on another day. Memory replayed the events as Bolan paddled on through the Idaho night.

He had left young brother Johnny in the care of the lovely Valentina Querente at the successful conclusion of that first Pittsfield blitz, dissociating himself from them out of fear for their safety. Desperate to get at Bolan, ruthless in their means of doing so, the Mafia would happily walk over Johnny and Val—if they learned of the love Bolan held for these two.

Not long afterward, despite Bolan's every precaution, the hideous nightmare came true.

Val and Johnny were kidnapped, their lives forfeit unless Bolan turned himself in to Boston *caporegime* Harold "The Skipper" Sicilia.

The "Boston Blitz" was a savage aberration in the Bolan crusade. Although Pittsfield had also been deeply personal, the only person in peril that time— aside from several dozen Mafia hyenas—was Bolan himself. But in Boston two innocent lives hung in the balance of Bolan's every move, and that fact was enough to drive him onward to mounting excesses in his furious rampaging search. This was the Executioner at the peak of frenzy, a primal driving force of raw ferocity not equaled again until Libya and Bolan's reaction to the discovery of Eva Aguilar's skinned-alive body—an aberration in a later war.

At a Mob hardsite in a Boston suburb, Bolan blew a Mafia confederation straight back to the Hell where it was spawned. In response, Skipper Sicilia sent the raging nightfighter a package, special delivery: the bodies of a young woman and a teen-aged boy, tortured and mutilated beyond recognition in ways that made it clear that death for these two had been a long-withheld blessing.

The Executioner became a desperate war machine in fury mode, a tortured soul acting out the only course of action that could ease his torment. In the following two hours, fifty-two Mafia bastards were consigned to eternity by his iron hand.

Only then did Bolan learn that the two "turkeys" were not Val and Johnny after all, but two other innocent victims of Mafia bestiality. In a tense mid-night confrontation on Boston Common, Bolan managed to elude a Mob suck-play and redeem the souls of the two people he loved—paying for them with Mafia blood.

In the small moment of calm when it was over, before the subsequent campaign in the nation's capital demanded the Executioner's flaming atten-tion, Bolan spoke with Valentina Querente for nearly an hour. When he left her, she was in tears, and his own face was a rigid mask of sadness and loss and re-newed determination.

He had given her back a normal life, while he would continue to wade through the gore.

He would never see her again, he vowed.

She was the first ally in the Executioner's home-front wars, perhaps even the first woman the lifetime professional soldier had ever loved. And for precisely these reasons, he gave her up.

Thousands of outlaws and violence-crazed radicals had died at his hand. Yet Bolan's proximity could inadvertently destroy the good and the sweet as well. For as long as the death vendors of the world had a price on Bolan's head, his touch was the touch of death.

Now Johnny Kerr had fallen as its victim, the innocent boy a lever in the hands of those who wished to topple the world. They would kill him without hesitation if they thought it necessary, or simply out of perversity if it were not. Johnny's life could be snuffed by the merest whim.

The Executioner meant to redeem that forfeit life.

With his own if need be. Indeed, if possible.

19

Bolan came rocketing through the pounding waves of the oddly named Dried Meat Rapids. Beyond it the river ran in a nearly straight line for a couple of miles. At the end of the run, just before the road to Riggins began, was a flat bench on the left bank called Long Tom Bar.

They were waiting for him there.

The chopper was a big Sikorsky S-76 Spirit, a turbo-prop transport that carried fourteen, including crew. It was parked on the narrow bar back toward the cliff, so there was room for another searchlight, which had been set up at the water's edge. Every thirty seconds or so it took a lazy recon upriver, as the assassination squad waited out its victim.

They had all the time in the world.

They had the boy.

Bolan began to stroke forward again. The next time the searchlight made its sweep, Bolan let it find him.

He closed his eyes tightly so his pupils would not contract. He could not afford to lose night vision even for a few seconds.

His combat sense remained on full alert through his self-imposed blindness.

The numbers counted down and ran out. Bolan stroked hard and slipped suddenly out of the light's grim stare.

A single auto-weapon spoke in raucous chattering chorus and a hailstorm of lead strafed the water where Bolan had been.

He paddled smoothly to the left bank and went EVA. A pair of grenades were nestled inside the half-zipped wet-suit jacket and he was carrying the M-16, loaded with the last full clip. He did not bother to conceal the Mirage but took cover a good 20 yards downstream from it, blocked out from the searchlight's scrutiny behind a flying-buttress protrusion in the face of the cliff that came down to the water's edge.

"Listen to me!" Sound filled the canyon. "A life depends on it."

The amplification of the battery-powered bullhorn made the voice sound scratchy, almost expressionless. Perhaps there was no expression in that voice to begin with.

"The firing just then was counter to my orders," the bland voice went on, accentless and yet somehow foreign-sounding. English was not this speaker's native tongue. "I want you alive."

Bolan snorted to himself in finely repressed rage.

"I won't try to mislead you. There is no point in us insulting each other's intelligence. I want some information—your name and the identities of your employers. When I learn what I want to know, you will die. How you respond to the questions will dictate the method of execution. If your answers are slow, so will be your death."

Bolan stood, cupped hands around his mouth and shouted above the river's noise, "Let me see the boy." At this first sound from him, the searchlight swept around in search of his position. But Bolan had already abandoned it and moved another several yards downstream.

Heartbeats thundered by, then the light moved again and ended up deflected straight down toward the sand of the bar on which it set. Johnny Kerr stumbled—or was pushed—into the circle of pale yellowness.

Even from where Bolan crouched, he could see that one of Johnny's eyes was bruised yellow purple and swollen mostly shut. There was blood on the boy's cheek and on the front of his wet suit. Bolan edged closer; the searchlight was about forty yards from his position, the last twenty across bare open sand. There were men clustered around the light's base. Bolan sensed rather than saw the others that guarded the chopper and the far perimeter.

Someone pulled Johnny back out of the light.

"His injuries are superficial," announced the flat voice that had to be Vigoury's. "He resisted, and he was beaten just enough to break that resistance, and no further. He will be all right."

"What do I do?" Bolan called, and moved again, though this time the searchlight did not seek him out.

"You give yourself for the boy."

"Don't do it!" Johnny's voice rang suddenly from the darkness near the light.

Bolan heard the soft thud of a fist striking flesh, a grunt of pain, then silence.

"What are your assurances?" Bolan called. He was close enough now not to have to yell, just at the edge of the dark half-ring of the sandbar.

"Myself," Vigoury said and stepped into the penumbra of the light, so his form but not his features were visible. "You have a weapon trained on me at this moment," Vigoury said. "You can kill anytime you wish—except that my men have you out-gunned ten to one, and once your muzzle flashes, you are dead as well. And so is the boy."

"Keep talking."

"There is another kayak on the beach." The light swept around to reveal it, immediately swept back. "The boy will go to it and remove downriver, un-molested. When he is out of range he will call out to that effect. The searchlight will immediately cover you, and you will lay down your weapon and turn yourself over to me."

"Agreed," Bolan called.

"No, no . . ." Johnny cried.

"Get moving, young John," Bolan said. "That's an order, soldier."

The night was becoming less dark by barely per-ceptible degrees. The lighted numerals of Bolan's chronometer read 0523. At his back, the eastern sky would be just beginning to go from dark black to smudged gray.

Bolan made out the vague shape of Johnny Kerr as he reluctantly crossed the bar to the water and set the kayak into the eddy. He braced the boat steady with the paddle and slipped into the cockpit, then pushed slowly off downriver.

"You have one minute, young man," Vigoury told him coldly. "If we do not hear your call by that time, we will proceed regardless. And we will take out the delay on your big friend here."

Johnny's paddle began to wheel steadily and the kayak disappeared into dusk.

Sixty seconds. Numbers and more numbers, always winding down toward the ultimate number: zero. One minute, an infinitesimal fraction in time's endless flow.

Sixty seconds as a prologue to death.

Bolan did not fear dying. How could he fear a companion who marched constantly at his side? But neither did he accept death—surely not in this place at this time, surely not at the hands of human maggots.

"Okay," Johnny's voice called. "I'm okay."

The sound came from too close. The boy had rushed it, out of fear for Bolan. The numbers were down and gone.

In front of the Executioner, the vague bulk of the big chopper lurked, and the ghostly forms of men drifted.

"Throw the submachine gun toward us," Vigoury ordered Bolan, and the searchlight came up to envelop him. The voice of the terrorist killer-for-hire was all steel now. "Do it!"

Bolan flung the M-16 by the barrel, so one man had to jump back to keep from being hit across the shins.

With the same motion his right hand dived into the wet suit and closed around the crosshatched casing of

one of the high-explosive grenades. He yanked the
pin in a practiced motion, diving out of the light and
swinging his arm in the same motion. He called out
the dreaded age-old battlefield warning.

''Live grenade!''

Weapons trained on him were momentarily forgotten as the group of men broke. Bodies lunged for the
sand.

The grenade's fiery explosion hurried dawn.

Most of Vigoury's men had gotten clear. One had
not and had been blown in Bolan's direction. The big
hellbringer ripped the M-16 from the dead guy's
shredded hands.

Bolan lay down an eight-shot ranging burst and
two forms keeled over. Answering fire racked toward
his muzzle flash and a slug nicked through the
neoprene of the wet suit's left arm, burning his flesh
below.

Bolan ignored it and stalked into the newest hellground, the hellground of the wilderness canyon.

His mind was clear of everything except the fight
and an unformed rage. It had to do with the boy, the
incarnation of another who also had been held hostage by savages.

The savages must die.

Two guys scrambled for cover behind the searchlight, bumping it so the beam swung wildly for the
sky. Bolan dropped prone in the sand and sent a
burst under the tilted light support. Hot 5.56mm
bonecrushers turned legs into twisted, mangled, useless stalks.

A guy broke for the water and Bolan hurried him

on his way. Lead punched across the guy's back and he toppled into the shallows along the beach, the upper half of his body in the river, staining the eddy's clear water with his rancid fluids.

The two backtrack guards had the cover of the rocks across the bar. There was no sign of Vigoury.

Bolan made the protection of the searchlight, careful to stay out of its beam. He felt for the switch, clicked it off so that his black-clad form returned again to the full embrace of the dimness.

One of the guys behind the rocks fired where the light had been, his slugs finding glass and metal above Bolan's position.

The line of rocks concealing the two guys was nearly fifty feet long, stretching from the water to the cliff-face. It was possible to circle behind them, but it would take too much time and care. If the gunmen were any good at all, they would already be moving to opposite ends of the line of rocks, looking to catch him in a pincer. He'd have to flush them before that happened.

But fate deprived him of the chance.

He started to rise from behind the spotlight's position, and a hand clamped around his ankle. Bolan stumbled and went down on one knee.

A shot whined by, screwing thin air where his head had been a fraction of a moment earlier. The ankle pull had just saved his life.

Bolan caught a glimpse of someone sprinting toward the chopper. But there were more compelling problems right now.

The guy behind him had lost a lot of blood from

his leg wounds, but somehow he had managed to retain consciousness. One hand held Bolan's ankle in a death grip. The other was bringing up an auto-loading pistol.

Bolan swung around the barrel of the M-16 and slammed it into the guy's wrist. The autopistol cartwheeled into the sand. Bolan wrenched free, lunged for it.

The guy with the mangled legs, and about half his blood puddled around him, tried to reach it, too, and lost the race. He gazed up and suddenly his angry grimace changed to an expression that was a mute plea for mercy, and Bolan gave it to him with his own gun, the hole clean and small and exactly in the middle of the guy's forehead.

Bolan only had time to fall prone again before the last two guys scrambled over opposite ends of the long rock wall.

He steadied the pistol in both hands as he tracked onto the nearer guy, the one at the foot of the cliff. They fired almost simultaneously. The other guy went on firing, the line of whining slugs walking toward and then away from Bolan's position, the last of them fired only by death reflex as the guy slumped back against the rock and then to the sand, the submachine gun finally silent in his lap.

Bolan whirled the handgun around toward the second guy.

And saw that the bolt remained open.

He had fired its last shot.

The moment was frozen. Bolan saw the guy's gun-muzzle pointing down at him, saw in the same sus-

pended split second his own M-16 lying only inches
from his hand but too far to reach in time.

A cacophony of full-automatic fire broke the moment, an untamed burst as a fully loaded magazine
was indiscriminately emptied.

But it was not the gunman who had fired.

Slugs raked up the length of the terrorist's body
and rose higher, ricocheting into the rock beyond
him, the muzzle-climb of full autofire pulling the last
few rounds into the sky.

When the guy went down, there was nothing above
his shoulders.

The firing stopped. At water's edge Johnny Kerr
stood over the guy who had tried to run, the dead
man's smoking M-16 looking too big in the boy's
hands.

Johnny stared at the headless torso away ahead of
him, and he audibly gasped.

Bolan rose to his feet.

At the same moment the chopper's engine roared
from idle to full throttle.

There was enough light to make out the expressionless features of the man sitting behind the
long sloping window of the helicopter's cockpit,
the features of a finely tuned killing automaton.

But the terror robot had broken down on the job.
Broken down with fear that contaminated the help-
less tissues of his inhuman heart. It was mechanical
surrender.

The chopper lifted itself clumsily from the bar,
and sand swirled in the rotor wash.

Bolan raked the cockpit window with the last six slugs in the M-16's magazine.

The chopper continued to rise.

Bolan dug into the wet suit, found the second grenade. His fingers sought out the pin.

He never had to pull it.

Seventy-five feet up, the chopper started to swing away to fly over them, and then aborted the moment before veering wildly in the other direction.

One of the rotors nicked the rock wall of the cliff. There was the loud *ping* of metal against rock.

For one sour beat the chopper hung in the air, virtually motionless. Then it plummeted.

Bolan sprang for Johnny. The boy could not tear his eyes from the man he had killed. His eyes were glazed with shock.

Bolan grabbed him up and threw him in the river's cold channel and plunged deep after him. He held on to the boy's wrist.

Behind them the Sikorsky plummeted into the ground with a racking yowl of rage as it tore at itself with its rotors.

Then it blew, the blast channeled riverward by the impenetrable cliffs.

Johnny's arm was limp in Bolan's hand, and he could hold him under no longer.

They were a good twenty-five yards downstream when they broke through the surface. Behind them, flaming wreckage crackled down through the dawn. An oily infernal torch streaked up the cliff-side. Another tank went off, and the torch flared anew into another fireball.

It was Hell greeting yet another day as Bolan finally made it out of the channel and dragged Johnny onto the shore.

Bolan flipped the boy on his back and began to apply cardio-pulmonary resuscitation, working rhythmically, methodically, calmly—and all the while fighting the franticness rising within him.

Yeah, Mack Bolan knew fear.

The boy's skin was cold.

Live, goddamn you, Bolan's mind screamed. How much death had he given this night? How could it be measured against this one life?

Johnny Kerr twisted. Water gushed from his mouth and nostrils. He half-opened his eyes, looked up at Bolan.

For a moment those eyes were crazed with fear.

"The bad stuff's over, Johnny," the big, gentle man said. "It's over for good now."

The boy struggled to sit up, and Bolan did not try to stop him.

Bolan stood, looked back upriver. The flames of the dying chopper were receding, and beyond them there was another light—paler, purer, full of life and hope. The leading edge of the new day's sun was peeking over the horizon ridgeline, far to the east.

"You did fine," Bolan said as he turned to the youth. "You did what had to be done."

"So...you're not mad at me?"

Bolan laughed. "Let's go home, brother John," he said.

EPILOGUE

The wall-mounted speaker in the War Room broadcast the sound of a scrambled phone-connection being broken, and the two sound-activated reel-to-reel tape machines clicked to a stop. The two people present sat for a moment without moving, as if unwilling to interrupt the tranquil silence of the dimly lit windowless chamber.

Then April Rose stood and shuffled the papers in front of her into an orderly stack. "I'll get started on the preliminary report right away," she said briskly.

"Good work," Aaron Kurtzman responded. "I'll begin inputting the raw data Mack just gave us, and see what matchups the computer finds."

"Fine," April said, and then her businesslike reserve broke down. "He's okay, Aaron," she almost sang with relief.

"For now, April," Kurtzman nodded sagely.

"Sure," she said, but her tone reflected obstinate joy.

Kurtzman dug out his pipe, frowned at it, changed his mind, returned it to the pocket of his lab coat. "There's still a price on his head," he said. "We must take it a day at a time, just like Mack."

"I know," she said softly. "Damn. Damn, damn, damn."

BOLAN AND JOHNNY had finally put out for good not long after dawn near the Partridge Creek Pack Bridge, because an old friend of the Kerrs lived on the road there. Her name was Mrs. Roberts, and she looked at the boy's bruises and scrapes and said simply, "Oh, my Lord."

"We kayaked down, ma'am," Johnny said. "Me and my friend here. I guess the water was a little high," he added, as if that were enough explanation.

"You're a reckless young devil, John Kerr," Mrs. Roberts said cheerfully and went off to find the keys to her pickup truck.

She drove them the last ten miles, all the while chattering without consequence, politely and typically refraining from asking questions.

The Forest Service Helitack Base and Pumper Station was just south of the little town of Riggins. There was an office building and a couple of bunkhouses, and two 4WD rigs with water tanks mounted on the back, awaiting the coming of the fire season. Everything was painted the requisite Forest-Service green. Across the river a lumber mill puffed white smoke into the cloudless sky. It would be a fine spring day.

Now, in one of the offices, Bolan hung up the phone and lit a cigarette. The conversation had lasted only long enough to calm April and to get the Stony Man base to set certain wheels in motion. Within a couple of hours a standby recovery-and-reclamation team ("The Housekeepers," they called themselves) would be on Salmon River, cleaning up the wreckage of men and machines strewed over thirty-some miles of the canyon. By next daylight there would remain little sign that the unspoiled wilderness had become a raging hellground for one long night.

The Housekeepers were a crucial element in the secret Stony Man counterterror enterprise, because a mop-up was in its way the grimmest job of the lot. Sometimes the housecleaning that succeeded Mack Bolan's own kind of cleansing-by-fire was left to local law-enforcement agencies, sometimes to the Farm's own federally subsidized specialists.

Back in St. Paul, on the mission to avenge the injuries of Toni Blancanales, the litter of smoking wrecked cars and corpses in the park had cast a cloud that had spread over the entire Twin City area; it had been dissipated only by police reassurances to the public that the mess was in hand and had been anticipated all along—which of course was a lie.

The devastation from the more recent doomsday in San Francisco had been sorted out by local administration in league with Stony Man.

Sometimes the hell was left vaguely visible for certain witnesses to savor. Thus the smell of cordite that hung over a small airfield in Bethesda, Maryland, was as instructive to foreign terror dealers as the wreckage of Mack Bolan's War Wagon in Central Park had been to organized crime.

Mop-up scenes from Florida to Massachusetts had conveyed subtle truth to curious international-terror intel feeds while concealing the true nature and extent of Phoenix's ongoing fire rain from the public at large, who remained eternally naive about the threat of terror that haunted the world with horror every day of the month, every month of every modern year.

In Idaho the call was for the cleansers to come running. Their mission would be a total wipe, to leave not a trace. Colonel Phoenix's HQ-coordinated strategy against a personal hit was now to keep low; no signs, no signals, just an emptiness to await his own pure explosion.

In the reception office the district ranger was hanging up another outside line. He gave Bolan a thoughtful look. "Never knew the bureaucracy to skeedaddle, Colonel, but I guess they did this time. Your chopper's waiting. Come back and visit us again sometime."

Bolan grinned, shook the man's hand and went out into the sunshine. The four-seater bubblefront helicopter was crouched in the middle of a grassy lawn in front of the office building. At its perimeter, a wind sock hung listlessly in the sunshine. Johnny stood beside the pilot, pointing at the chopper, asking something. Bolan, like any man, envied the kid the resiliency of his youth. The younger man already was rebounding; time would pass and the very worst would be eventually forgotten, or at least erased in terms of the smell, the hellish sounds, the chilling, unnerving stops to time.

The flight upstream took less than an hour; the river unrolled below them like time running backward. And when they landed at the east-end helitack base at Indianola, the chopper's skids settling soft as snow onto the rich spring-green grass, the river meandering slyly by as if denying the wild white water awaiting just downstream—as Bolan looked on the wild peacefulness, it seemed for a moment as if daylight had actually blotted out the reality of their firestorm gauntlet run.

The pilot and his two passengers stepped down onto the gloriously green sward.

"There's a Forest Service truck waiting to drive young Mr. Kerr into Salmon, sir," the pilot said, winking at the youth. "Another one of our boys will retrieve the rental vehicle left at Corn Creek and your river gear, and see that it all gets returned.

"I'd appreciate it."

"Radio message came in just before we landed. It said a jet will rendezvous with you at Maelstrom AFB in Great Falls, Montana at 1100. I'll be flying you up there myself, sir, right away. We're just here to deliver the boy."

"Right," Bolan said. "Give us a minute, would you?"

"I'll grab myself a cup of java. Can I get you one for the flight?"

"Sounds good."

Bolan and the youth moved to the edge of the landing pad, far enough from the chopper not to have to raise their voices over the engine's idle. Johnny kicked at the grass and looked down at the sluggish river. "There's no point to me going into that hospital in Salmon," he said for the third time that morning. "I been hurt plenty worse than this."

Bolan placed a hand on his shoulder. "It's just a checkup, Johnny. You'll be out of there in a few minutes. The truck will wait for you."

"I'll go," Johnny relented. Then he grinned a teenager's kidding smile. "But I'm blaming it on you."

Immediately his expression turned grave again. "What happened last night...all those men trying to kill you.... I guess what you do must be pretty important."

"It is to me, John."

"I...I guess it's pretty secret, too—never mind, that's okay. Folks'll be talking, though, what with that boathouse gone and all...."

"I wouldn't ask you to lie, John."

"I won't. But that doesn't mean I have to go shooting off my mouth either."

"That's right. Good man. Just one thing. Miss Poten back at the Gold Bar Creek general store knows me as John. Okay? From now on you and me share the same name."

The boy smiled—then asked the question Mack Bolan had been dreading.

"Will I see you again?"

Dreading it because Bolan wanted badly to say "yes." The deadly night they had shared had forged a bond between the two of them that could never be broken, and Johnny Kerr had become in some ways as dear to Bolan as the other Johnny he resembled. Mack Bolan and Johnny Kerr were now brothers as well, brothers in blood, linked for all time by the withering assault they had faced—and resisted—and turned back on itself.

Together.

Yet now more than ever, the nourishment of the companionship of his fellow citizens of a world that he fought to preserve was forbidden to the dedicated warrior. A calculated effort had been made to assassinate him. It would not be the last. As always, anyone close to him would be in mortal danger.

To be friend to The Executioner was like being chained to a cement block and set adrift on a raft in an endless stormy sea. Sooner or later the raft would break up, and the weight would drag you down in the blackness, and the fathomless depths would swallow you whole.

"No," Bolan said, simply but with aching sadness. "I'll never forget you, however, brother John Kerr."

The youth moved away from the rotor-wash as Bolan turned his back and stepped toward the helicopter. Johnny watched the craft lift off, his face bright, his arm up in a salute and then a wave.

For one final time Bolan let himself remember the other Johnny. The young Kerr boy had given back to Bolan a part of that brother he had had to abandon, had let him have a few too-short hours of kinship once more. For that Mack Bolan would owe Johnny a debt too great to be paid in any one lifetime.

No, perhaps there was a way he could pay it, at least in part. He could fight on, fight to preserve the cosmic balance of the world through which the man John Kerr would soon walk.

And that man would be like the boy: courageous and true and large.

He would care.

Bolan brought up a salute, sharp and correct, to the figure on the ground, and the chopper slewed around on the pivot of its rotor and climbed beyond the ridge, and the boy disappeared from view.

"Continental Divide off to the right, sir."

The pilot's voice crackled in his headset, and Bolan automatically looked in the direction he was pointing.

He found tears of pride and sadness clouding his vision.

MACK
BOLAN

THE EXECUTIONER 51

appears again in
Vulture's Vengeance

Mack Bolan knew it was now or never-never land as he reached for the ejection-seat handle. He rocketed into the night above the exploding fighter jet...and directly into the path of his pursuer's lead-spitting plane.

Even if he reached the ground alive, the madness would not be over. It had only just begun....

Flying into the face of terror, Bolan takes to the skies in *Vulture's Vengeance* to rip through adversity and snatch supreme success!

Mack Bolan's

ABLE

AN EXECUTIONER SERIES

TEAM

by Dick Stivers

In the fire-raking tradition of The Executioner, Able Team's Carl Lyons, Pol Blancanales and Gadgets Schwarz are the three hotshots who avenge terror with screaming silvered fury. They are the Death Squad reborn, and their long-awaited adventures are the best thing to happen since the Mack Bolan and the Phoenix Force series. Collect them all! They are classics of their kind! Do not miss these titles:

#1 Tower of Terror   **#3 Texas Showdown**

#2 The Hostaged Island **#4 Amazon Slaughter**

Watch for new Able Team titles
wherever paperbacks are sold.

GOLD
EAGLE

Mack Bolan's
PHOENIX FORCE
AN EXECUTIONER SERIES
by Gar Wilson

Phoenix Force is The Executioner's five-man army that blazes through the dirtiest of encounters. Like commandos who fight for the love of battle and the righteous unfolding of the logic of war, Bolan's five hardasses make mincemeat out of their enemies. Catch up on the whole series now!

"Expert...well-versed in antiterrorist tactics and paramilitary matters.... Realism and Detail!"
—*Mystery News*

#1 Argentine Deadline   **#3 Atlantic Scramble**
#2 Guerilla Games   **#4 Tigers of Justice**

Watch for new Phoenix Force titles wherever paperbacks are sold.

GOLD EAGLE

MACK BOLAN

THE EXECUTIONER SERIES

I am not their judge. I am their judgment—I am their executioner.

—Mack Bolan,
a.k.a. Col. John Phoenix

Mack Bolan is the free world's leading force in the new Terrorist Wars, defying all terrorists and destroying them piece by piece, using his Vietnam-trained tactics and knowledge of jungle warfare. Bolan's new war is the most exciting series ever to explode into print. You won't want to miss a single word. Start your collection now!

"Highly Successful" —*The New York Times*

#39 The New War
#40 Double Crossfire
#41 The Violent Streets
#42 The Iranian Hit
#43 Return to Vietnam
#44 Terrorist Summit

#45 Paramilitary Plot
#46 Bloodsport
#47 Renegade Agent
#48 The Libya Connection
#49 Doomsday Disciples
#50 Brothers in Blood

GOLD EAGLE

Available wherever paperbacks are sold.